Pandemonium of Parrots

Dawn Treacher

Stairwell Books //

Published by Stairwell Books
161 Lowther Street
York, YO31 7LZ

www.stairwellbooks.co.uk
@stairwellbooks

This is a work of fiction. Names, characters, businesses, places,
events, locales, and incidents are either the products of the
author's imagination or used in a fictitious manner. Any
resemblance to actual persons, living or dead, or actual events is
purely coincidental.

Cover art: Dawn Treacher

ISBN: 978-1-913432-55-3
p7

Also by Dawn Treacher

To my mother, Pamela Taylor
for all her encouragement and support in my writing.

Table of Contents

Chapter 1 – The Orangery

With a sweep of its wings the mechanical parrot flew from Otto's hands. It curved higher, its blue tail feathers catching the light. Otto watched the parrot glide through the puffs of white that belched from the cloud machine as it swooped across the orangery, joining the others that perched high in the branches of the orange trees.

Climbing back down the ladder, Otto wiped a smear of blue paint onto his trousers. This last mechanical parrot looked even more majestic than the others. Otto had concentrated really hard, his tongue clamped between his teeth as he painted the slender lines of the tail feathers and the turquoise plumage on its breast. His uncle, Delderfield Macauley, had sat scrutinising every last stroke.

Otto pulled off his neckerchief and used it to wipe the back of his neck. Small droplets of moisture had formed on the inside of the windows and he felt a draft of cool air. The orangery was a magnificent domed glass conservatory bursting with life. It had been built on the side of an austere grey bricked house, the largest in a row of terraced houses, that sat at the end of a street in Brummington.

Turning around, Otto noticed a long crack had split the blue tinted glass. He pushed aside the leaves that sprouted from a banana palm and traced his finger down to a large hole that had been cut in the lowest glass panel. It was hidden behind rubber plants and lush green ferns. Air from outside wafted through the hole, bringing with it the smell of smoke and rancid vegetables. It was an air tinged with the dirt of streets and factory chimneys. The leaves nearest the hole shivered in the cold draft.

Otto's oldest memory was a journey through the cobbled streets. It had been a cold November afternoon, and Otto could not have been more than five years old. It was the complete lack of colour that Otto remembered the most, shades of dirty grey and black, just like the sky where thunder clouds gathered. That was seven years ago now and he hadn't stepped outside the orangery since. He'd almost forgotten what it was like outside, how the grey smog smothered everything it touched.

The hole in the glass was large enough for him to crawl through, if he had the mind to and Otto wondered what could possibly have made it. He peered through it. Beyond came the sound of wooden carts splashing through puddles, the horses' hooves clipping cobbled stones. A thick smog hung close to the street that wound its way past huddled terraces. Children shouted in the gutter against the chime of the factory clock.

He pulled his head back inside. It was only then that he noticed the girl crouched between the ferns, hunched over a notebook, a piece of charcoal clutched in her grubby hand. Her ragged, mouse-coloured hair flopped over her face as she worked busily across the white paper, capturing the parrots in a few strokes, smudging their plumage with her little finger.

"What are you doing in here?" said Otto, grabbing the notebook from the girl's hand.

"Give that back," cried the girl, pushing her hair out of her eyes and adjusting a small pair of round glasses on her nose.

"Who are you?" Otto looked at the picture the girl had been drawing. She had caught the movement of their wings, the glint in their glass eyes. "Did you make that hole?"

"What if I did?" She snatched back her notebook, stuffing it inside her dress. "I'm Florence, what's it to you?"

"If my uncle finds you, he'll..."

"Let him. See if I care."

Florence crawled back through the hole where the thick, smelly air had already begun to hide her legs.

"Parrots aren't black," called Otto, as Florence turned to leave.

"Well there ain't any colour out here."

"Don't go," said Otto. Florence had already started to walk away, the bottom of her dress soaking up the water from the cobbles, her hands thrust deep into her pockets.

"Will you come back to finish it?" called Otto. He hadn't spoken to another child for so long he didn't really want her to leave. Otto looked at his blue fingers, the paint still sticky. "I could get you coloured paints," he shouted. Florence kept walking, kicking a stone so hard that it clattered down the street.

Behind Otto, the parrots squawked in unison, their heads bobbing up and down, their gold metal claws shuffling them along the branches as they sang to each other. The sound of water trickling along a tropical river burbled out of a gramophone above Otto's head. The heady citrus of oranges swamped the air. Pushing the leaves back into place, Otto crawled out into the centre of the conservatory, picked up the ladder and made his way to the doorway. He tossed his thick mass of black curls out of his eyes as he struggled to get the ladder through the door.

Otto didn't hear the lorry that drew up outside or the footsteps that walked close to the large wood panelled door with the golden knocker shaped like a parrot. Only one of the parrots saw the three faces against the glass and no-one heard the voices that whispered to each other.

Chapter 2 – What the Monkey Saw

"Ah Otto, there you are. I've been meaning to talk to you."

Otto entered his uncle's workshop, squeezing past a large potted palm and a row of lemon trees. The humidity in the cluttered room brought Otto out in a sweat and he could feel a trickle running down his neck.

"I'm expecting a delivery later, I'll need your help to carry it in." Delderfield Macauley didn't look up. He squeezed the monocle in his right eye as he carefully aligned the cogs in front of him and inserted a tiny golden screw. "These flamingos are proving tricky. Their knee joints need to be looser and their feet wider to allow them to wade."

Otto watched his uncle assemble the large bird. Delicate legs supported a body covered in a mass of intricate metal plumage. The flamingo's glass eyes still lay on the work bench, and Otto was sure they were watching him.

"Uncle, could I go outside this morning? I'd be back in time to help you."

Delderfield Macauley dropped the screw in his hand with a tinkle. "What did you say?"

Otto stuffed his hands in his pockets and kicked the potted palm with his foot. "I thought I could go outside, just for a walk and..."

"Really! Have I taught you nothing? Look around you at all I have created. Who needs to go outside when everything of beauty and colour is here?"

"It's been a long time," said Otto. "I wouldn't go far."

"No, I won't hear of it. It's far too dangerous out there."

Delderfield Macauley got up from his chair. He wiped his greasy hands on a rag. Otto's uncle towered above him, his purple silk waistcoat straining over his rotund middle. As he spoke, his bushy moustache shook, sending spit flying. "You're safe here, away from the grime and prying eyes. The answer is no and that's final."

"But you go out. You've travelled the world..."

"That's just it my boy. I have recreated here all the wonderful things I found on my travels, so that you and I no longer need to. Now come, surely you haven't finished the tasks I set you today? We need more clouds. Crank up the machine, boy."

With that, Delderfield Macauley dismissed his nephew, turning his attention back to the flamingo. "Oh, and on your way out, wind up the monkey for me."

Otto looked around him. In his uncle's workshop the shelves were crammed with mechanical creatures waiting to be painted and repaired. A row of tiny humming birds sat silently next to a toucan which lay on its back, its feet up in the air, its wing broken. A stack of paint pots cluttered the floor and a tin of paint-stained brushes sat beside them. More brushes spilled out onto the floor.

On a small cabinet on the wall sat a spider monkey. White fur sprouted from its head and framed its black eyes. Otto had to stand on tip toe to reach it. Turning it over, he wound the key in its back until it would go no further. The monkey turned its head, blinked its eyes and clapped its tiny hands together. Its porcelain teeth chattered. Otto's uncle sat hunched once more over his work and he didn't look up when Otto popped the monkey on his shoulder, letting it coil its slender black tail around his neck. Carefully, Otto grabbed two small pots of paint and a brush.

The monkey wound the handle of the cloud machine. Otto peered out through the tinted blue glass of the orangery. He could see only outlines and shadows of the world outside. The monkey chattered loudly as the chimney belched puffy white clouds up into the air where they bobbed and floated out across the orangery. The parrots squawked. Otto couldn't stop thinking about Florence. He wished he hadn't been so rude. What if she never came back?

Otto pushed his way back through the banana palms and left the pots of red and orange paint on the ground by the hole in the glass. He balanced a brush on top. He was about to walk away when he changed his mind. He squatted down on the ground and prised one pot open. Dipping the brush into the red paint he painted the word sorry on the glass, as if writing in a mirror so it could be read on the outside. Then he pushed the lid shut.

Outside the hole he heard voices. They muttered so quietly that he couldn't catch what they were saying. He peered out. There he saw three pairs of legs, each wearing a pair of dirty black boots, with rusty metal buttons. Otto pulled his head back inside and held his breath. The boots were edging slowly around the outside of the orangery.

The monkey crawled onto his lap and popped its head through the hole. Only the monkey saw the faces of the three men who were paying such attention to the orangery, but of course it couldn't tell anyone.

Chapter 3 – The Delivery

The bell above the front door clanged.

"Otto, come and help me," called Delderfield Macauley, unlocking the wooden door.

Carrying the monkey on his shoulder, Otto walked into the hallway past the gallery of photographs. There were pictures of tropical islands, lagoons and mountains and one of his uncle standing on a large sailing ship. Beside it was a picture of two small boys standing on a large rock on a beach. Light shone through the arched glass ceiling of the walkway, glinting on the glass of the frame.

Vines crawled over the walls, their stems weighted with bunches of black grapes. Otto picked one as he made his way along the black and white tiled floor to the front door which stood open, a huge potted tree on the threshold. His uncle, crouched low in his tweed trousers, struggled to lift the terracotta pot and after several moments he dropped it on his toe.

"Quickly my boy, before I break something."

Otto took one side and together they manoeuvred the pot along the hallway. With the tree safely rested on the floor, Otto could see through the open door. A row of plant pots sat on the doorstep. Beyond them he saw a large grey lorry. A stocky man, his head plastered with greasy black hair with a neat parting combed through the middle, was lifting another palm tree from the back of the lorry. His grey overcoat bore years of grime and a rip along the hem. His black boots were old and worn with rusty metal buttons. Another man stood in the back of the lorry but Otto could only saw his hands, dirt encrusted under the nails and a large gold signet ring on his little finger. A third man sat in the cab, tapping the steering wheel, whistling. The man's cap was pulled down over his eyes so far that only his bulbous nose was visible beneath it.

The monkey ran along the hallway and sat on the doormat chattering loudly. It pointed at the man outside.

"Will you get a move on," said Otto's uncle, "And get that monkey back in here."

Otto picked up two large pots of flowering shrubs. A grey wind buffeted their pink orchid flowers and their glossy leaves shivered in the cold. Otto nudged the monkey back inside with his foot as his uncle handed the black haired man a pile of gold coins. As the door was closing, Otto saw the lettering on the side of the lorry.

Hodge and Sons

"Stop gawping and help me with these," said his uncle, carrying an armful of pots out into a small back room lined with work benches already overcrowded with plants.

"Uncle, where did these plants come from?" They seemed so out of place in the grey street. The terraced houses were so crowded together that not a single blade of grass grew.

"Shipped into the port specially they were. It took quite some organisation to get them here too. Now to get them warm before they die of cold."

"But… I really would like to…"

"No time to talk my boy, lots to do. Remember, I'll need your help to paint the first of the flamingos later."

Otto left his uncle spraying the plants with a fine mist, fussing over their leaves and muttering to himself. Making his way back into the orangery, Otto wondered if Florence had come back.

The monkey swung down from a palm tree, chattering noisily as if trying to get Otto's attention. A parrot glided across the orangery, its metal wings spread wide. Otto pushed his way back to the hole in the glass. His face broke into a smile when he saw Florence with a

16

notebook on her knees, paintbrush in hand. The girl didn't look up but carried on sweeping red paint across the parrot's wings, dotting the plumage on its tail feathers.

"I'm sorry about earlier," said Otto, breaking the silence.

"That's okay," said Florence, opening the orange tin. "Thanks for these."

"Where did you learn to paint like that?" asked Otto, sitting down beside her.

"I've always drawn things, comes natural like. First time I've ever used paint though."

"What's it like outside?"

"What do you mean?" Florence looked up, dropping the paintbrush on the ground beside her, where it splodged orange paint.

"I haven't been outside for years," said Otto.

"Why not?"

"My uncle doesn't want me to go outside. He says everything of beauty and colour is here and he insists it's dangerous out there."

"It can be, you just need to know how to keep your head down, that's all. Nothing to it really."

Otto picked up the paintbrush and put it back on the pot of paint. Florence blew on the page of parrots until the paint was dry to the touch. Then she folded the notebook and tucked it back inside her dress.

Florence got up to leave.

"Can you show me?" asked Otto.

"Yeah, if you like. Won't your uncle miss you?"

"Not for a while."

Together the two of them crawled out through the glass, stepping into a pool of swirling smog that loitered over the damp cobbled road. Only the monkey saw Otto go but it wouldn't have told anyone, even if it could.

Chapter 4 – The Factory Gates

Florence led Otto along the street of tightly packed terraces. Dirty grey washing strung between their windows. A skinny dog sniffed around a lamppost. A group of children chased past Otto, laughing. The leader, a boy with a face as dirty as the pavement, held a paper parcel tucked under his arm. His boots were so worn his toes peeped through. Behind them the thrill of a whistle rang out. Heavy feet pounded the cobbles. Florence grabbed Otto's hand and pulled him into an alleyway, pinning him back against a stone wall. The children shrieked and the dog howled.

"Not a sound, do you hear me?" hissed Florence.

The children were swallowed by the shadows. The wall of the alleyway was damp against Otto's back. His thin shirt offered no warmth against the cold, sooty air that swirled up around his feet, sending goosebumps down his arms. A huge factory chimney pumped black smoke into the air which was dragged across the streets by a gust of wind that bit into Otto's skin. He shivered. His heart beat loudly in his ears.

"What's happening?" whispered Otto.

"Just some kids trying their luck. Best keep outta the way."

"What do you mean?" Otto peered around the corner but the children had gone, all but for one shoe that lay on its side in a puddle.

Doors slammed. Otto watched a steam carriage drive away, its metal cog wheels spinning, a huddle of top hats just visible under the taut black canopy.

"Guess they got caught thieving stuff," said Florence. "Nothing to do with us."

"Who was chasing them?" Otto glimpsed a face peering out of a doorway, a pair of eyes watching silently.

"The Brigade, nothing gets past them. Come on, the coast's clear."

"But where did the children go?"

Otto kept close as Florence led him down the alleyway where doors with peeling grey paint guarded small stone yards.

"They'd have taken them to the workhouse most likely. I might see them later when I head back. At least they'll get fed tonight." Florence pulled Otto along. "You've got to stop asking so many questions. Like I said, to survive 'ere you 'ave to keep your head down and mind your own business."

Otto did his best to keep up with Florence who darted down a side street. A damp chill and stale stench made Otto shiver even more. He pushed his hands deep into his pockets to keep warm. They kept in the shadow of a vast windowless brick building which ran the length of the street behind a pair of ginormous gates. Above its walls rose huge chimneys belching smoke in a continuous stream that covered everything it touched in a film of grit and grime. It hurt Otto's eyes and stung the back of his throat. The wrought iron gates spelled a name.

Macauley and Brothers

Otto stopped and blinked smoke from his eyes.

"We gotta keep moving, we don't wanna be caught hanging around 'ere."

"But..." Otto pointed to the gates.

"The factory, what of it? Anyone who can work ends up there. The weaving machines run day and night. Guess that's where I'll be soon enough unless I go to sea first."

"But the name..."

"Macauley, your uncle." Florence yanked Otto's arm. "You telling me you didn't know how your uncle affords that fancy glass house of his?"

"No," said Otto, rubbing his eyes. A piece of grit was making them water. Otto had never asked. He knew his uncle was an inventor, his passion for mechanical animals was his life but...

"I've 'eard of children going in there and never coming out again. Some say they get stuck up the chimneys, others say they get caught under the machines. I'd rather take my chances at sea."

Otto blindly let Florence lead him. He no longer noticed the streets they walked down. He stared at the cobbles and the rivulets of dirty water that trickled along beside them. A black rat scurried down the edge of the pavement.

Rounding a corner, Otto tasted salt in the air. The wind blew through his hair. It no longer smelled of smoke but of something different altogether, a pong of seaweed and rotten fish. The dirty smudge of green on the horizon was the swell of the sea. He heard the cry of gulls circling the boats that rocked in the harbour. Water slapped their wooden hulls.

"One day I'm gonna catch a ride on one of those steam boats," said Florence. "Might even get myself a voyage across the Pantatlantic ocean."

Florence perched on the sea wall sketching the sails of a large ship. Wooden oars jutted out of portholes along its side and a carved wooden figurehead of a woman with flowing hair looked out to sea from its bow. A huge metal propeller struck out beneath her and vast sails projected like wings from either side of the ships belly.

Unlike the white fluffy clouds that pumped out of the cloud machine in the orangery, the ones above Otto were a sheet of steel grey. Even the churning sea was almost black. Otto realised what Florence had meant when she'd said there was no colour out here.

Florence shut her notebook and jumped down from the wall. "I'll finish this later. Best get you back before your uncle misses you."

Florence steered Otto away from the sea. If they'd turned around they would have seen a large grey lorry pull up alongside the sea wall bearing the name Hodge and Sons. They may have seen three men enter the Black Horse Tavern, gold coins burning a hole in their pockets.

Chapter 5 – And Then There Were Five

Otto was relieved to be back inside the orangery but he couldn't stop thinking about the sea. He had vague memories of being aboard a ship when he was very small but he'd persuaded himself that it must have been a dream. But the smell of the sea and the swell of the water were hauntingly familiar somehow.

"Otto, is that you?" called his uncle.

Otto sat on a wooden slatted chair, the monkey curled up on his lap, enjoying the warmth on his face.

"No time to laze around my boy, it's time to wind the parrots before they drop off their perch."

The monkey leapt from Otto's lap and swung up into the palm tree overhead. Otto stood up.

"Uncle..." He wanted to ask his uncle about the factory but how could he do that without revealing he'd betrayed him?

"Whatever it is I don't have time, there's simply too much to do." Delderfield Macauley took a small gold tin from his waistcoat pocket. He opened it, took out a pinch of snuff and snorted loudly. Then he pulled on the gold chain of his pocket watch, opened its case and tapped the dial. "Is it that time already? I really must be going. I have a call to make but I'll be back before tea. Now get winding, my boy."

Otto watched his uncle leave. So did the driver of a grey lorry parked outside the orangery.

Otto grabbed a long handled fishing net. There was a rustling and Florence appeared through the banana leaves.

"You all right? You didn't say much on the way back."

"I was thinking, that's all," said Otto, "Thanks for taking me outside... it's just... I didn't know about the factory and..."

"Don't matter. Guess you'd have found out soon enough. Why the net?"

"It's time to wind the parrots. The tricky bit is catching them," said Otto, raising the net high above his head and sweeping it across the orangery. He scooped up one of the mechanical birds. He lowered the net, untangling the squawking parrot from the mesh. "Hold this will you?," said Otto, passing the net to Florence.

Squatting down, Otto held the parrot firmly in his lap and turned the small brass key that was set in the parrot's back.

"Did your uncle really make these?" said Florence, crouching down to see the parrot more closely. The bird turned to face her. Its glass eyes moved, watching her intently.

"Of course," said Otto. "He's made the monkey too and lots of other birds. He's making a pair of flamingos at the moment."

"They're beautiful," marvelled Florence, stroking the parrot's colourful, intricate feathers. "Folk always wonder what Delderfield Macauley does, locked away in his glass house. Some say he's eccentric, shut away like that. Many think he's got something to hide."

Otto released the parrot which flew back up to the orange tree where it perched squawking, as if to warn the others.

"One down, five to go," said Otto.

Florence helped Otto until they'd wound five parrots but when Otto searched for the last parrot it was nowhere to be found.

"Can you see it?" asked Otto, pushing back the banana leaves and peering through the ferns.

The monkey chattered loudly, pointing towards the room where Otto's uncle looked after his new plants.

"It won't be in there," said Otto, but the monkey chattered louder still, then scampered over to the door, pushed it open and disappeared inside.

Otto and Florence followed. Inside, the workbench was piled high with plants, terracotta pots and heaps of soil. There was no sign of the parrot, just a small mechanical snail that traversed the bench slowly until the monkey patted it to the floor. A draft blew in through an open window. Otto could see the street outside. He heard the trundling of a wooden cart and smelt the splash of rain on the cobbles.

"Do you think the parrot escaped?" Otto pulled the window shut. " Uncle never leaves windows open."

"This was no accident," said Florence, examining the window. The metal catch had been sheared off. "That's the sign of a thief. Your uncle's been robbed!"

"You think someone took the parrot?"

The monkey jumped up and down, gesticulating excitedly at the window. There, caught in the frame was a single orange feather, the metal bent out of shape.

Chapter 6 – Then They Were Gone

When his uncle returned that evening, Otto didn't mention the parrot or the broken window but he'd made sure to close it shut. He'd stood plant pots in front of it to hide the broken catch. He was sure his uncle would find a reason to blame him. Florence had promised to look out for anything suspicious. As it happened, Delderfield Macauley was far too busy to notice: it was time to paint the flamingos.

"Now remember, the paint needs to be just the right shade. Not too pink and not too orange."

Otto carefully mixed the paint but his mind was elsewhere. What if whoever took the parrot came back for more?

"Watch what you're doing my boy, you're getting paint all over the floor."

Salmon pink dripped from Otto's brush. The monkey was restless. Instead of sitting in his usual place up on the shelf watching, he paced up and down, chattering, his tail curled high in the air. At intervals the monkey would vanish down to the orangery then return to pace again.

"There's something wrong with that monkey," said Delderfield Macauley, putting down his paintbrush. "Come here little chap, let's take a look at you." But as Otto's uncle reached out to grab the monkey it screeched and ran along the workbench, then leapt to the floor. The monkey ran out into the orangery and scaled the tallest tree. There it sat for the rest of the afternoon.

Otto wished he could check on the parrots too but it would make his uncle suspicious. He daren't draw his uncle's attention to them.

At last the flamingos were finished. The pair stood on the workbench, the paint on their feathers still glossy and wet. Otto's uncle admired the long sweeping curve of their necks.

"Excellent. I can't wait to get the pond installed my boy and after that... What do you think? Oh I know, silver and gold mechanical fish to swim in the pond. Why didn't I think of that sooner? So much to order and so much to do."

Otto desperately wanted to check on the parrots but his uncle, ravenously hungry after all that painting, tucked into an enormous tea of fish paste sandwiches, onion soup and griddled scones. Otto only picked at his hoping Florence might have news.

It was only when his uncle had gone for an afternoon snooze that Otto got a chance to go into the orangery. He counted, hoping somehow that the missing parrot would have returned, but no. There were still only five parrots and no sign of Florence either.

Otto may not have felt able to tell his uncle about the stolen parrot just yet, but he was determined to do everything he could to stop any more parrots being stolen. So after his uncle retired to bed, Otto sneaked back into the orangery and checked the remaining five parrots were safe in the trees. Each sat silently, their metal eyelids closed. Otto went to the broken window in the potting room and as he couldn't fix the window, he shut the door to the room and stacked a pile of wooden crates in front of it. The crates were heavy with pots of paint, pieces of metal and junk his uncle hadn't got around to clearing out. Soon Otto had barricaded the door so well he doubted anyone could get through it if they ventured through the window again.

Worried by the hole in the glass of the orangery, Otto piled a crate of terracotta pots in front of it. He'd move them in the morning so Florence could get back in. Otto then made himself a bed of sorts outside the potting room door with two wooden slated chairs and a pile of blankets. He settled down for the night to keep watch. The monkey curled up around Otto's neck.

The clock ticked past midnight, then one o'clock, then two.

Everything was dark. Both Delderfield Macauley and Otto were sound asleep. The monkey kept watch, though as the hours passed he wound down so much that his eyes closed. No one heard the footsteps in the orangery or the squawk of the parrots.

As the clock struck six, Otto awoke with stiff legs and a dull ache in his head. He wound the key in the monkey's back. The monkey chattered and sat up. The barricade of crates still sat, undisturbed and the door to the potting room was shut, just as Otto had left it. Sleepily, Otto walked into the orangery. The monkey sprang from his shoulder and climbed along the boughs of a tree and there it let out a terrific screech.

The parrots had gone. Every last one of them.

There was no time to wonder how to tell his uncle. On hearing the screech, Delderfield Macauley came running, still in his flannel dressing gown, the cotton cord trailing along behind him. When he realised his parrots were missing, he started to shout.

"All that work, stolen. My beautiful parrots, who would do such a thing?" His words turned to tears.

Otto was speechless.

"Get out of my way, boy!"

Otto's uncle ran through the house, his hair wilder than Otto had ever seen it. He knocked over a potted orchid and threw open the front door. "I've been robbed!" he bellowed into the street. "Fetch the Brigade!"

Otto thought of the hole in the glass and ran to the orangery, pushing his way through the banana leaves. His heart fell as he saw the wooden crate now lying on its side and the pots smashed on the floor.

"Otto! Where are you?" yelled his uncle.

Hearing feet running down the hall, Otto rushed back to the front hall. Two men, each dressed in black with top hats on their heads, barged past him, knocking a picture to the floor where it smashed into a shower of glass. Outside in the mist of morning, Otto saw the black steam carriage of the Brigade parked just by their door. In a panic, he headed back to the orangery. He watched in silence as the Brigade searched for clues. The monkey clung to his shoulder, baring his porcelain teeth.

And then, they found the hole in the glass. The pot of paint he had forgotten to remove had spilt in a large pool and orange footprints crossed the floor. That's when the barrage of questions began. Otto thought they'd never stop.

He didn't want to, but Otto was forced to tell them about Florence, even though it made his uncle shout even louder. He wished he'd told his uncle about the first missing parrot but he just couldn't bear it. What did it matter now?

"Well, this Florence is obviously the thief," cried Delderfield Macauley. "What are you waiting for, find her and arrest her, immediately."

"But she wouldn't..." said Otto, as the men from the Brigade ran from the house and thundered off in the steam carriage in a cloud of smoke soon swallowed by the mist.

"How could you?" cried Otto's uncle. "How could you lie to me like that?"

"But I..."

"Go to your room this minute!"

But Otto didn't go to his room. Instead he sneaked into the potting room and opened the broken window. Somewhere out there were his uncle's six mechanical parrots and if he didn't do something his only friend, Florence, would be taken away. From what he'd already seen, Otto would probably never see her again and his uncle would never let Otto outside anymore. He knew he had to find Florence before the Brigade did. Otto climbed outside, taking the monkey with him.

It was the monkey that spotted the blue tail feather lying on the cobbles next to a pair of large orange footprints.

Chapter 7 – A Clue

Otto hurried down the street keeping in the shadows of the terraced houses. He was grateful he'd grabbed his uncle's jacket as needles of rain pelted his face. He turned up the collar. The monkey chattered, tucked inside the front of the jacket, with only its tail stuck out of the bottom.

Otto hurried past the factory gates, not daring to look up or linger. His uncle would be furious when he discovered Otto wasn't in his room, but what did it matter now? All Otto could think about was Florence. It was all Otto's fault. What if he didn't find Florence before the Brigade did? He wondered what the Brigade did with suspected criminals.

The smell of the sea blew towards him as he headed out towards the harbour. The boats rocked on the sea's mighty swell, the wind billowing their sails. A clip clopping of hooves and the crack of a whip startled him. A dappled grey mare trotted past him, a wooden cart rattling along behind. The driver gripped the reigns. His eyes were perched above a red veined nose. Bushy sideburns smothered his cheeks which were red raw from the wind. He starred at Otto. The monkey stuck out its head.

"Get back inside," whispered Otto, turning to face the wall. "Or everyone will be staring at us."

A throng of men shuffled along the path next to the sea wall, pipes clamped between their lips. Smoky tobacco mixed with the salty sea spray. Otto tagged along behind them. He tried to convince himself that no-one would pay any attention to just another boy. He was just another boy in the harbour, no different than the children kicking a cabbage along the sea wall and throwing stones into the angry white waves. Only the mechanical monkey was out of place. Instinctively, Otto wrapped his arms around his front, squeezing the monkey close to him, its soft fur pressed up against his chest.

He scanned the harbour, hoping to see Florence finishing her sketch but there was no sign of her. Gulls squalled around a fishing boat that surged into the harbour.

Otto noticed something lying on the ground near the sea wall. It was Florence's notebook, the edges of the pages turning soggy as the rain grew heavier. A stick of charcoal lay crushed into the cobbles. Otto picked up the notebook and tucked it into his jacket pocket. He headed away from the harbour, checking to see if anyone had noticed. He kept on walking, rain trickling down his chin until he came across a narrow alleyway, where he turned, away from watchful eyes.

Under the shelter of a doorway that had long since been boarded up, he took the notebook from his pocket. There was the drawing of the parrot, flying across the page and the ship bobbing in the water. The next drawing was of a man who was stocky and dressed in a long overcoat worn over big buttoned boots. The man's face was framed by hair slicked down from a centre parting. The monkey popped its head out of Otto's coat and chattered loudly, tapping the page with its finger.

"I know, I've seen him too," said Otto. "I'm sure he came to the house, delivering plants to Uncle." But where had Florence seen him and why had she drawn him?

Otto turned the page and something fell out from between the leaves and clattered to the ground. The monkey sprang after it and plucked a small red metal feather from between the cobbles.

"It's a parrot feather," said Otto, taking it from the monkey. "Where could Florence have found it?"

Hearing footsteps, Otto tucked the notebook and feather into his pocket and ran back to the harbour. Florence had to be there somewhere unless...the Brigade had already taken her. If they had grabbed her, like those other children, Otto might never find her.

29

Florence had mentioned a workhouse but Otto had no idea where to start.

Otto pushed the monkey back inside his jacket. "Stay there and no peeking."

All Otto had left of the mechanical parrots were two feathers. He knew he couldn't go back to the orangery now, not without the birds. The group of children were still playing by the sea wall.

"Have you seen a girl called Florence?" called Otto.

Two small boys in ragged long shorts shook their heads. A girl, with chestnut hair pulled tightly into two bunches, balanced on the sea wall skimming stones into the waves.

"What about her?" she called.

"I'm looking for her and..."

"Don't go telling people that, the Brigade just took her." She skimmed another stone which skipped along the surface four times before disappearing under the crest of a wave.

"Where did they take her?"

"Reckon they'll 'ave taken her to the Magistrates Office. I don't fancy her chances. It ain't the first time she's been taken there."

"Where can I find it?" asked Otto.

"Why do you wanna know?" said the girl, looking round.

"I have to talk to her."

"They won't let you if they 'ave her down the cells." She pointed away from the harbour. "It's down past the Black Horse Tavern, second street on your left."

"Thanks," called Otto, turning to leave.

"If you see her, tell her she stills owes me. May as well pay me too as they're sure to hang her. She won't be needing it were she's going."

Otto didn't get a chance to ask her name. A loud bell rang out, startling the gulls into the air, and the girl ran after the boys who were heading in the direction of the factory gates.

Chapter 8 – The Escape

Otto headed back towards the Black Horse Tavern, pushing his way through a crowd of sailors that had been expelled through the doorway along with a cloud of stale tobacco smoke and the sour reek of beer.

"Look where yer going."

"Get outta the way!"

A pair of rough hands pushed Otto backwards. He shrank back against the tavern's wall, letting the crowd elbow past him and stagger down the street. Their voices were carried with the smoke in the wind, and they were soon obliterated by the sheet of rain that relentlessly pounded the cobbles.

Otto pulled the oversized jacket up over his head, making sure the monkey stay tucked inside and he ran away from the Tavern.

Following the girl's instructions he took the second turning on the left, past a row of blackened terraces until he reached a tall stone building set back from the street behind shiny black railings. Above an arched iron gate a lamp kept watch. Stone steps rose steeply to an imposing black door with a polished door handle and a bell pull. The rain had begun to ease and stepping over a large puddle, Otto peered into a small window beside the door.

Sure enough, inside he could see the top hats of the guards of the Brigade. This had to be the right place. Not wanting to be spotted, Otto crept round the side of the building where a row of windows dotted the long grey stone wall of the Magistrates Office. He squeezed through a gap in the railings. These windows were thick with grime. Otto wiped the first window clean with the sleeve of his uncle's jacket until he could see inside.

A man with a pair of horn-rimmed spectacles balanced on the end of his nose stood behind a large wooden desk in a tiled entrance hall. He was writing in a ledger, dipping his pen into an inkwell to replenish the nib in between entries.

The sound of a steam carriage thundering to a halt outside the main entrance made Otto jump. In a panic, he spotted a small set of steps that led down below street level to another window that was barricaded by metal bars. He ran down the steps. The window must have looked into a cellar but the glass was so thick with soot that Otto couldn't see inside. He heard the carriage door whir open. Otto ducked down in the shadow of the railings. The monkey squirmed its way out of the tweed jacket and tried to crawl onto Otto's shoulder. Otto hugged the monkey close to his chest.

"Not a sound, do you hear me?"

Someone must have yanked the bell pull for a peal rang out. In the silence that followed, Otto was surprised to hear his uncle's voice. The monkey wriggled free from Otto's grasp and sprinted round the side of the building.

"Come back," whispered Otto. Peering around, he could see the entrance door. There stood his uncle, a black cloak glistening with rain draped around his shoulders.

Otto reached out, grabbed hold of the monkey's tail and bundled it back. The monkey chattered excitedly, pointing.

"I know, it's Uncle," said Otto. "It means Florence must be here somewhere but you have to keep out of sight."

With a jangle, the door to the Magistrate's Office swung open and Delderfield Macauley stepped inside. The monkey grew more and more agitated and wouldn't stop struggling. The door sprang open again and this time two guards dressed in black stepped outside. With a screech, the monkey broke free from Otto's clutch, scampered up the steps dodging the men's feet and darted in through the door of the Magistrate's Office.

"Come back," called Otto, but the monkey didn't hear him and even if it had, it wouldn't have listened.

"What the...!"

The guards spun around, running inside to see what had nearly tripped them over.

"Did you see that?"

"It looked like a monkey."

The door slammed shut behind them leaving Otto outside in the street. He didn't dare try to follow. He went over to the window beside the door and from there, he caught a glimpse of the monkey darting across the entrance hall. It raced over the man's desk, knocking over the inkwell and disappeared down a tiled corridor out of sight. Otto saw the surprise on his uncle's face.

"Now look what you've done," sighed Otto.

With such a commotion in the entrance hall there was no way that Otto could get inside unnoticed. All he could do was wait. He heard his uncle shouting.

"What about my parrots?"

Otto wondered if his uncle had recognised his own monkey but maybe he hadn't, as the monkey had run by so fast.

Otto stood there awkwardly, not knowing what to do. He couldn't just leave the monkey inside. The drizzle of rain soaked into his hair making it frizz into even tighter curls than usual. He shivered as he sat near the cellar window sitting on the steps, the tweed jacket wrapped tightly around him. And there he stayed for what seemed like forever until he heard a tapping sound. It was getting louder and more indignant with each sharp clack, and was coming from a window on the floor above. Otto scrambled up the steps and looked along the row of windows until he spotted the monkey, hanging out of one of the windows, tapping it with a bunch of metal keys.

On tip toes, Otto managed to heave himself up through the window. The monkey chattered incessantly.

"You've found Florence, haven't you?"

The monkey nodded.

"Show me the way then." Otto wasn't at all sure that this was a good idea but the monkey was already standing in a long corridor, tail held high, holding a bunch of keys in one hand. Otto heard footsteps coming along the hall and a door slamming in the distance. The sound echoed along the eerily empty corridor.

The monkey scampered over to the top of a flight of steps that led down to what must have been the cellar. It didn't wait for Otto. The monkey sprinted down them, dragging the keys behind.

"Hey! Don't make so much noise, they'll hear us."

The monkey had already rounded a bend in the steps.

"Where did you get those keys?"

The monkey just laughed while running so fast Otto struggled to keep up. The steps led them down to a dark corridor, lit only by a small gas lamp on the wall. It threw the monkey's shadow across the hall. Three doors stood in a row. Footsteps pounded the floor above and Otto could hear the guards calling.

"They went this way."

The monkey stopped outside the second door and reared up on its hind legs chattering urgently.

"Give me the keys then," said Otto. "How do you know it's this door?"

The monkey tapped its nose and jumped up and down. Otto was beginning to realise that his uncle's mechanical animals were so much more than he had ever imagined. No wonder he kept them locked away.

By the time Otto tried the third key his heart was pounding in his ears and he was sure they would be discovered. The key turned in the lock with a click and the door swung open. Inside sat Florence, hunched on the floor, drawing in the dirt with her fingers.

"How did you find me?" said Florence looking up. Her face burst into a grin.

"I'll tell you later," said Otto looking over his shoulder. Footsteps clattered on the stairs at the end of the corridor. "We need to find another way out."

"I know the way," said Florence, leading Otto and the monkey back out into the corridor. She raced long the corridor and round a sharp bend. Otto wrapped the monkey around his neck and clung on to him tightly. Florence skidded to a stop.

"We can't get out!" panted Otto. Behind them the guards were closing in.

They'd reached a dead end. The wall in front of them held one small window and it had no latch.

"Get back here!" yelled the guards.

Florence snatched the bunch of keys from Otto's hand and swung them at the glass repeatedly until ... Crack! The glass broke. With her elbow Florence punched out the remnants which fell to the floor in glistening shards.

"They're over there!" bellowed a voice behind them.

"That monkey stole my keys. The girl is gone!"

"Follow me," said Florence climbing through the window, her elbow dripping blood. "It's a bit of a squeeze."

"But..."

"Just get a move on. Pass me that monkey."

Otto did as he was told. He clambered through the window, ripping a hole in his uncle's tweed jacket. He tumbled out onto the cobbles next to Florence and the monkey.

A whistle rang out and another steam carriage screeched to a stop.

"Stop them!"

That was his uncle's voice.

"And get that monkey!"

"Run," yelled Florence, grabbing hold of Otto's arm.

"But where?"

"Up there of course," said Florence, pointing to a metal ladder that ran up from the street to the very top of the building, three stories up.

"I can't..."

"You can! Just don't look down. "

The monkey jumped onto the ladder, its tail held high to balance it and off it climbed. "You next," said Florence. "I'll be just below you."

Otto climbed the ladder, the wind blowing in his face, raindrops settling on his eyelids. He felt all of his blood drain down to his feet. He gripped the ladder so tightly that his fingers went white, but he kept climbing until they reached the roof.

"Up you go," said Florence, pushing Otto from behind until he was sat on the tiled roof. The monkey chattered beside him. Florence walked along the ridge of the roof, balancing expertly with her arms spread wide. "This way," she called.

Otto wobbled with every step he took and was convinced he was going to fall. He reached a chimney and grabbed hold of it and there he froze. Everything below him spun round in a blur of brick and smoke. Gulls screeched overhead. Only the monkey saw the sea on the horizon and the hull of the metal galleon steaming into port, the skull and crossbones flying from its mast.

Chapter 9 – Wanted

Otto couldn't hear the voices down below any longer, just the pounding in his ears as he wriggled along the ridge of the roof, his hands clasping the wet slate tiles, his legs straggling the roof. The monkey trotted along ahead.

"Not much further," called Florence.

"What if they follow us?" asked Otto, his teeth chattering in the cold wind. He looked straight ahead, not daring to look down at far-away cobbles, in case the world started spinning again.

"Nah, you won't get that lot climbing up here. Anyway, why did your uncle send the Brigade after me? Because I broke the glass?"

Otto stopped. The wind buffeted his face. He felt a trickle of sweat run down his forehead and settle on his eyebrow. "The parrots... They're all gone and..."

"All gone? Well that's something. But why me?"

Otto shuffled forwards again to the next chimney where he sat and rested. He drew his legs up to his chest, his back against the chimney. The rooftops around him swayed unnervingly.

"They found the hole and the paint... I had to tell Uncle about you and..."

"Oh I get it. He reckons I'm one of those lost causes and a thief with it."

"I..."

"So what? I steal food when I'm hungry and sometimes things of value but I didn't steal those parrots. What would I do with them?"

"I know it wasn't you," said Otto. "That's why I..."

"I didn't nick them but I did see something."

Otto remembered something and reached inside his jacket pocket. He held the notebook out to Florence.

"I found this in the harbour. That man you drew, he was one of a group of men who delivered some plants for my uncle."

Florence stuffed the notebook inside her dress. "I saw him, he had a parrot, stuffed into a bag it was, and he was going into the Black Horse Tavern. He dropped something..."

Otto took the red feather from his pocket.

"Yeh, that's it."

"I reckon it belongs to one of those parrots. Maybe the first one that was stolen."

Florence looked in front of her, into the rainy fog. "We have to get down from here. I know somewhere, it's not far. If you can step over that gap up ahead we'll be nearly there."

Florence took Otto's hand and guided him along the roof until they reached the end of the building. Across a foot gap was another building made of sooty brick. "I've got you, don't look down and jump when I say jump."

"Where are we going?"

"Somewhere the Brigade won't be looking. You'll get used to it, and once you stop thinking about it, it comes easy. Now jump."

Otto had never been so scared before. He steadied himself on the roof of the next building, and he really did think he may be sick. The smell of the sea steadied him. It was odd. The more he inhaled salty air, the more it brought back memories he couldn't begin to explain.

"One more jump, we're nearly there."

Hand in hand they jumped to a lower roof. Below them a dormer window jutted out. Its frame was rotten and its glass broken. Florence swung herself down and slipped inside like she'd done it loads of times before. Florence pushed the window wide open and grabbed the monkey, pulling it inside. She called up to Otto.

"Lower yourself down backwards. I'll grab your legs."

"I'll fall," cried Otto, feeling his legs dissolve beneath him.

"I reckon you're just going to have to trust me or stay up there forever," laughed Florence.

Turning around, Otto's hand slipped on the wet tiles and he felt himself falling. The tiles were cold against his cheeks. Florence caught hold of Otto's legs.

"Grab onto the frame and in you get. Can't have you landing in the street, you'll give us away."

Inside the building, Otto lurched forwards and his legs gave way. He landed in a heap on bare wooden floor boards. The monkey jumped onto his lap, clapping its hands. Otto was relieved that the room was no longer moving. He was sitting in the attic of a house. A pile of wooden crates were stacked in one corner, shrouded in cobwebs, but across the room, Florence sat on a makeshift bed made of stained, ripped blankets and straw. A candle sat in a dingy, old glass jar next to a pile of notebooks and the last crust of a loaf of bread.

"You said you lived in the workhouse," said Otto.

"Well I did... Once. I like my own space, that's all."

The monkey sat on Otto's shoulder, looking out of the window. Footsteps stopped outside on the pavement below. Otto listened.

"Where do you reckon they went?" came a voice.

"Dunno, but it looks like they're in it together," said another. "Check the workhouse for that lass Florence in case she goes back there. They can't have gone far and a few gold coins will soon loosen some tongues."

Florence squatted down on the floor with her notebook in her hand. "Best stay here for a while."

"We have to find those parrots... or my uncle will never forgive me."

"We're not going anywhere. We'll sit tight." Florence opened the notebook and began to draw.

Outside, the monkey saw a grey lorry drive past. A man in a black uniform pasted a poster to the window across the street.

Wanted:
Information about a girl and a boy in connection with the disappearance of six mechanical parrots.
Reward: ten shillings.

The monkey curled up around Otto's neck and closed its eyes.

Chapter 10 – The Black Horse Tavern

Evening slipped into night and the gas lamp from outside threw weak shafts of light across the wooden floorboards. The monkey lay lifeless on Otto's lap. He turned the monkey over and wound its key until it flicked its tail and rolled open its eyes. The monkey's ghostly porcelain teeth chattered in the dark.

Otto nudged Florence who was snoring steadily. "We can't just stay here."

"What..." stammered Florence, sitting up and shaking her head.

"I don't like it here," said Otto, trying not to sound as frightened as he felt. It was so very different from his own room, but how could he ever go back? His uncle would be furious.

Florence jumped up and looked out of the window at the slither of the moon that hung like a shard of glass in the sky.

"Time we were going."

"Where to?" said Otto, following Florence down a creaking staircase. Its steps were so rotten in places that Otto was sure he'd fall through them at any moment.

"To the Black Horse Tavern of course. Those so-called delivery men are up to something. Reckon they're your thieves. Regulars at the Tavern too I shouldn't wonder."

"We can't go in there," said Otto, jumping down the last step and trailing after Florence into a large empty room at the back of the house. The monkey sat high on Otto's shoulder, its tail wrapped around Otto's neck.

"If you want to find those parrots you will. I reckon we're both in heaps of trouble anyway."

A broken window was set in the back wall, the gaps letting the bitter night sneak in.

"I know a way in round the back. The cook has a soft spot for me see. With so much waste no one notices a few scraps going missing and she loves my pictures."

Outside in the back alley, the cold sliced through the button holes of Otto's tweed jacket. The wind snatched Florence's words. Otto tried to keep up, his teeth chattering as much as the monkey's. He heard raucous laughter spilling out of the Black Horse Tavern long before he saw it up ahead. Firelight flickered in the windows and the smell of smoked kippers seeped out of the front door along with the voices of drunken sailors. The tavern's sign squeaked on its hinges.

Florence led Otto away from the harbour. They nipped through a hole in a fence which led them to a narrow alleyway. At the end of the alleyway stood a door. Florence pushed it open.

"Keep that monkey quiet."

The door to the tavern's kitchen stood ajar. Florence pulled Otto inside into a sweating fog of heat. Fish sizzled in skillets and plumes of steam billowed above large tin pans over an open range. The cook, a huge red-faced woman, stirred a vat of boiling water and didn't look up. The smell was so delicious that Otto's empty stomach grumbled. In amidst the clatter of pots and pans, Otto and Florence scooted around the kitchen and out into a dimly lit corridor.

"Stay close," said Florence. "It's packed tonight, they'll barely notice us if we keep quiet and anyway most of them are too drunk to care."

Otto, feeling more out of place than ever, pulled up his collar and shrank down inside his uncle's enormous jacket. He squeezed the monkey who lay deep inside. Pipe smoke stung Otto's eyes and made him cough. Florence glared at him.

Fishermen, sailors and factory workers pushed and shoved to reach the bar which was already two rows deep. Florence pulled Otto through the crowded room, skirting between tables where card games were in full swing and arguments were erupting between glugs of ale.

"Over there," pointed Florence.

By a bay window, in the light of a candle that dripped down a glass bottle, sat a man Otto recognised. Florence had captured his likeness well in her sketch. The man's two companions looked familiar too. They were the men who'd delivered his uncle's plants, he was sure of it.

"That's them," whispered Otto. "What do you think they did with the parrots?"

"Stashed them somewhere, I guess."

A flash of gold caught Otto's eye. What looked like a lizard slithered between the legs of a stool. The creature's intricately articulated mechanical tail swished from side to side as it moved. Cogs whirred in its legs. A pair of green glass eyes blinked.

A hand grabbed the lizard and stuffed it into the pocket of a long leather coat. The coat was worn by a stout, squat figure who appeared to be female, in tall leather boots laced up to the knees. Otto couldn't see much of her face, which was obscured by a pair of metal goggles buckled around a head of thick red curls. The lizard popped its head out of her pocket and flicked out a metal tongue. The woman heaved open the tavern door and was swallowed by a crowd outside. The door slammed shut behind her.

From where Otto and Florence huddled, they caught snatches of conversation.

"Gotta move them tonight."

"The ship's docked in the harbour."

The men's stools scraped the floor as they got up to leave.

"Let's follow them," said Florence.

Judging by the number of empty tankards on their table, the men had been in the tavern a good while. They swayed as they stood up to leave. One of them knocked over his stool, sending it clattering across the floor. For a brief second, the man with slicked-black hair stared in Otto's direction but seemed to look straight through him.

"Move, now," nudged Florence.

Squeezing past an empty table laden with the remnants of a greasy fish supper, Florence grabbed half a kipper before darting out of the tavern door. Otto followed, feeling the blast of night air sting his face. Outside they ducked behind a stack of wooden barrels. Otto crouched

41

beside Florence. The smoky kipper smelt divine. He couldn't remember the last time he'd eaten anything. Florence ripped it in two and passed half to Otto. The monkey, still hidden in Otto's coat, wriggled free.

They didn't have long to wait as a minute later the three men emerged from the tavern, their feet just inches away from where Otto sat swallowing the last morsel of kipper. He could see the man's buttoned boots with a splash of orange paint on the toe. His dirt encrusted trousers were tucked inside. The monkey pointed excitedly.

The men were heading back towards the harbour, their ale drenched breath hanging in the night air above them as they sang so loudly they drowned out the footsteps of the monkey behind them.

"Oh there be gold a plenty,
and rum to warm you to your boots,
but keep away from the pirate
or he's sure to cut your throat."

Florence and Otto followed at a safe distance, keeping the monkey in their sights. The ink black sea tossed many a sailing boat around, dwarfed by the hulls of huge steamships, their rigging painted silver by the light of the waning moon. Only the monkey saw the skull and crossbones flapping in the squally wind. Otto and Florence never took their eyes off the three men who trudged along the harbour and down a deserted alleyway.

A rat streaked across Otto's path. Up ahead, the alleyway opened up into a cobbled street littered with abandoned lobster pots and rope coiled like slumbering snakes. The splintered hull of a fishing boat was home to a skinny stray dog. The whites of its eyes followed Otto's and Florence's every step. Otto shivered.

The three men stopped in front of a row of wooden sheds. The man with a gold signet ring squeezed on his chubby finger fumbled with a padlock and rusted chain on the shed in the middle.

"What the...?" He threw the broken lock to the ground and wrenched open the shed door.

"Who the heck...?"

"We've been robbed!" bellowed the man with buttoned boots. He grabbed a lantern, lit the wick and hoisted it aloft. There sat the grey lorry. The light flickered on the name painted on its side, Hodges and Sons.

The monkey clambered up the shed door and sat at the very top, swinging its tail. The lorry doors were open and inside a bundled pile of canvas, Otto saw flashes of blue, red and orange feathers like jewels in the dark.

"The parrots!" Otto gasped.

"What the..." The man with the golden ring rummaged through the pile of sleeping parrots.

"Let me see," yelled the man with a bulbous nose, a cap pulled down over his head so far that Otto couldn't see the rest of his face.

"1,2,3,4,5... There's one missing!" he bellowed.

"You stupid idiot, you couldn't have locked up properly."

"It weren't me. I did, I know I did."

"That lock's been broken, it ain't no accident."

The three men shouted at once, each blaming the other. One pushed another.

"The sneaky blighter! I said you should never trust a pirate."

One of the parrots moved its head and blinked an eye. The others had wound down hours ago. The monkey clapped its hands over its mouth and shook its head.

Chapter 11 – The pirate

"A pirate?" whispered Otto.

The monkey ran along the roof of the wooden shed and down to where Otto and Florence hid in the shadows.

"I heard whispers of a pirate in the harbour," said Florence. "Goes by the name Jethro Silver. Only has one eye, so they say, because a shark ate the other. Wanted for piracy across two continents."

"Have you seen him?" Otto's uncle had told of many voyages across the oceans but he'd never mentioned a pirate.

"Nah, but I saw his galleon, steaming across the sky. It had masts as tall as houses and it has seen the blood of a hundred sailors wash across its deck."

The lorry's engine started and its doors slammed shut. The monkey chattered loudly. With a crunch of its gears, the lorry reversed out of the shed and bounced along the cobbles. Its headlamps threw a sickly yellow light across the puddles.

Otto watched the lorry drive away with the five mechanical parrots stowed in the back.

"We have to follow them," he called out to Florence, jumping up.

"You'll never catch 'em, but I know where the pirate ship is alright," said Florence as she started running in the direction of the harbour.

Otto scooped up the monkey and chased after her. He splashed through the puddles, back past the scrawny dog who now trailed behind him, following the scent of greasy kippers that still stained Otto's fingers.

The harbour lay deserted, sleeping in the moonlight, the water rocking the steamboats anchored there. At first Otto didn't see the ship, but then he spotted it at the far end of the harbour. It was a vast galleon, its masts so tall that the crow's nest disappeared into the swirling mist that shrouded it like a curtain.

"There," pointed Florence, leading Otto out along the harbour.

The skinny dog stopped to scavenge. A pile of wooden crates spewed fish heads and crab claws. The giant galleon loomed above Otto, dwarfing all the other steam ships moored around it. Its rigging was silhouetted by the moon like charred bones that rattled as the sea lapped the galleon's hull.

Otto kept walking. The monkey jumped onto the sea wall and scampered along it, tail held high.

"What if the pirate sees us?" called Otto.

His uncle's library held many books about ships but only one made mention of a pirate ship. Otto remembered reading it. That night his sleep had been stolen by nightmares, punctuated by vivid snatches of a pirate; someone who slit the throats of sailors and plundered their ships. When the nightmares came back day after day it was always the same image which haunted him. A pirate slashing the air with a cutlass and a scream ringing out, so terrible that it made Otto stuff a pillow over his ears.

"You won't find the parrot back there." Florence stood beside the enormous galleon. She beckoned Otto to hurry up.

Otto remembered the words of the girl throwing stones over the sea wall. They hang thieves, if she were to be believed. If they didn't find his uncle's parrots, the gallows were waiting for Florence. Otto wasn't sure what terrified him more; coming face to face with a steam pirate or watching Florence hang. Otto shivered. He was about to catch up with Florence when he heard footsteps behind him.

The monkey let out a screech. Beside it on the sea wall slunk the golden lizard, the very same lizard Otto had seen in the tavern.

"If you're looking for a parrot, I can help you."

Otto spun round. Behind him stood the woman from the Black Horse Tavern, her goggles zooming out to get a better look at him.

She clicked her fingers and the golden lizard crawled towards her. She plucked it off the sea wall by its tail and swung it into the pocket of her leather coat.

"But... Who...?"

The woman's goggles whirred back into place, making her red curls quiver.

"I know your uncle, Delderfield Macauley."

"You do?"

Florence hissed at Otto.

"Your friend's right. I'm sure Jethro Silver couldn't resist such a fine parrot. In fact, I saw him, nothing much escapes me."

The woman leaned nearer to Otto, her goggles zooming out quite alarmingly so that they were just inches away from Otto's face. "I saw him in the tavern. Yeah, he had it stuffed in a sack but there's no mistaking a parrot's squawk."

She spotted the monkey.

"Come here little one." She reached out her hand to where the monkey sat.

The monkey raised itself up on its haunches and bared its porcelain teeth in a furious chatter before running along to the wall to where Florence stood waiting.

"Such a shame about Natisha. She was a genius of course. Who else could spark such intelligence in a mechanical creature? Poor Delderfield could only ever hope to copy his twin sister."

Otto froze. All Otto had left of his mother was a faded photograph which he kept under his pillow. She stood with the ocean behind her, wind blowing through her hair. His uncle never mentioned his sister, not for many years, and Otto had long since stopped trying to ask questions.

"Follow me. Jethro will be addled by rum by now."

"Really?" Florence looked questioningly at Otto, but all Otto could hear was the name Natisha swimming round inside his head.

Otto let the woman lead them alongside the slumbering galleon and climb the creaking gangplank to the deck.

Only the monkey saw the grey lorry pull up beside the harbour and the three men bundle out a large canvas sack. Otto was already half way up the gang plank when the three men dragged the sack behind them and onto the deck of a small steamship which rocked in the swell of the sea, the words Golden Serpent painted along her side.

46

Chapter 12 – Emoria Cogwright

Up on deck, Otto felt the galleon shifting beneath him but it wasn't the rocking of the ship that was making his stomach churn. Whoever this woman was, she knew his mother.

"Who is she?" hissed Florence, as they crept along the deck, the wind tapping out a tune on the rigging above them. The huge sails pulled like sheets on a washing line trying to escape.

Otto shrugged.

"I saw her in the Black Horse Tavern," whispered Otto. He scooped up the monkey. The churning of his stomach was making him feel sick.

"Can we trust her?" whispered Florence.

"She knows my uncle." Otto couldn't bring himself to mention his mother.

Snores echoed below deck.

"Stop your whispering and keep close," called the woman, heaving open a hatch set in the middle of the deck. "Don't be fooled, pirates have a sixth sense. He'll know we're here all right. We get in and out, no dawdling, not if you want to see tomorrow."

Otto's heart thumped loudly.

"Who are you?" he said, his voice trembling as much as his hands.

The woman spun round, her goggles zooming out towards him to see him better.

"You're not as stupid as I thought you were. Trust no-one, that's my motto. The name's Emoria, Emoria Cogwright. Me and Jethro Silver go way back. He'd slit your throat in a heartbeat if he thought you had something he wanted. He has no crew, they never live long enough and anyway he doesn't need them. He's no ordinary pirate."

Otto's skin shivered. Florence's eyes grew wide.

"We go below deck and we snatch that parrot. Not a sound. Don't even think. He can hear your thoughts and predict every move you make. If he comes after you, run like your life depends upon it. Which it will."

The monkey trembled. Otto squeezed it tightly.

Emoria started climbing down the ladder. It was dark below deck, the gloom filled with a fug of rum and bad breath. Otto followed, clinging to the wooden rungs, Florence so close behind him that Otto could feel the warmth of her breath. The monkey wrapped itself around Otto's neck like a muffler.

The snoring grew louder the lower they climbed and the clanking of the rigging beat as loudly as Otto's heart. It took a few seconds for his eyes to adjust. They were in a corridor in the bowels of the galleon. The sea slapped relentlessly against the hull. It was so airless that Otto felt sicker than ever. He followed Emoria's footsteps towards a cabin door which creaked open on its hinges, a slither of candlelight deep within.

Through the open cabin door, Otto could see the parrot sitting on a perch inside a large metal cage. The parrot watched them intently across the cabin. Gently, Otto put a hand over the monkey's mouth to keep him from making a sound. The cage stood on a wooden desk. Scrolls were heaped high at one end next to a plate of bread and stinky cheese. A map was stretched open, weighted down by a brass eyeglass and compass. A lantern swung overhead, its candle burnt down almost to the wick, its light flickering across the darkness.

A barrel of rum lay on its side, a trickle of amber liquid dripping onto the floor, leaving a sticky pool. An empty tankard rolled beside it. Dingy velvet drapes hung around a wooden bunk behind which came the snoring, as rhythmic as the rocking of the galleon. Sticking out of the end of the bunk were a pair of feet wearing large leather boots buckled to the shin. Resting on the floor lay a cutlass, its blade caught by the light, sharp enough to slit a throat in a single swipe. Otto's mouth was so dry he could barely swallow.

Emoria pointed to the cage and Otto nodded. She nudged the cabin door wide open with her foot. The snoring faltered. Otto tip toed across the cabin, praying his footsteps wouldn't betray him. Florence waited by the door, fear flickering in her eyes.

Otto picked up the cage. It was heavier than he'd expected and the weight of it made him gasp. His foot slipped in the puddle of rum. The parrot squawked. Florence caught her breath. The snoring stopped and Otto's heart missed a beat. He shot a look at Emoria just as the velvet drapes were swiped aside and a hand grabbed the cutlass. Emoria withdrew a musket from the pocket inside her coat. She raised it in front of her, its black wooden handle in her hand and her arm steady. In that second, Otto ran.

"Get back here!" boomed a deep voice behind him. The pirate, already on his feet, swaggered towards the cabin door, reaching it in a single stride.

Florence was already climbing back up the ladder, with Otto close behind and not daring to look back.

"You!"

There was scuffle, and then a musket shot rang out followed by the sound of splintering wood.

"Don't be so surprised, Jethro. It was only a matter of time."

Florence helped Otto scramble up on deck, hoisting the parrot's cage out in front of him. The monkey leapt from Otto's shoulder and ran along the deck. Emoria emerged through the hatch, musket in hand. Otto could hear her heavy breathing and smelt the musket powder in the air.

"Now give me that parrot!"

Emoria reached out to grab it from Otto. The parrot flapped its wings, squawking loudly. The monkey shrieked. Jethro Silver loomed up behind behind Emoria. Otto swung the cage out of Emoria's reach. Florence grabbed hold of his hand and pulled him along the deck, stumbling as they ran.

"No you don't, not this time!" yelled Jethro Silver.

Otto couldn't run any more. His legs ached and he couldn't stop shaking. He leaned against the rail of the galleon. The cold night air hurt his chest as he fought to catch his breath.

Jethro Silver, all six foot four of him, towered above Emoria Cogwright. One eye was stitched shut, a deep scar cutting across his face. His skin was weathered by years of wind and sun. His face was framed by a mass of black curls, some so long they twisted down his back like a horse's mane.

He stood, feet planted apart, his thigh length leather coat as creased as his skin. He wore a brown leather holster strapped around his chest and a belt tightened with a large metal cog as a buckle. Around his neck he wore a chain. On that hung a delicate latticed locket which rested against the rough cloth of his tunic. Otto stared at it and felt his blood drain from his face. He knew the picture of his mother by heart, every detail from her blonde tousled hair and rose bud lips to the locket she wore around her neck.

"Don't take what's not yours," cried Jethro Silver.

"That never stopped you," laughed Emoria, swinging around to face him.

Otto thought his legs would buckle.

Chapter 13 – Otto's Surprise

"Run," whispered Florence in Otto's ear.

"I can't," said Otto. He could no longer control his feet, let alone run. Something of his mother's hung around the pirate's neck and the smell of the galleon was unlocking a memory he could barely grasp hold of. He didn't like the way Emoria had tried to snatch the parrot or the way the monkey had screeched. When Jethro Silver noticed Otto there was a noticeable shift in the pirate's glare.

"Got yourselves some fellow thieves, Emoria?" he sneered. He raised the cutlass out in front of him and met Emoria's stare. "I took you for working alone."

"Like you, Jethro?"

"Just give me back the parrot and we'll call it quits."

"You know I can't do that," said Emoria, edging backwards to where Otto steadied himself at the side of the galleon.

Florence breathed heavily beside him. "Now," whispered Florence, grabbing Otto's arm.

Otto tried to run but the parrot flapped around, making the heavy cage sway.

"Stop right there," bellowed Jethro Silver.

The cutlass sliced through the air, flying in an arc above Emoria's head, sailing past Otto's ear. Florence pushed Otto to the ground, knocking the cage to the deck, springing open the catch. The cutlass juddered to a stop, wedged into the mast beside them. The parrot, taking its chance, flapped its wings furiously and flew out of the cage. It flew higher and faster. The monkey chased after it but the parrot swept up to the top of the mast and there it stayed. The monkey scaled the mast, just like an orange tree and the parrot screeched.

"Never trust an accomplice," sneered Jethro, pushing past Emoria and pulling his cutlass free from the mast. He waved the cutlass in front of him, jabbing the air. "You best be leaving."

"Not empty-handed, Jethro, that parrot is mine. I've been waiting a long time," Emoria laughed. She aimed her musket at a pile of wooden barrels stacked on the deck and fired. As the top barrel ruptured with the shot, it fell, knocking over and sending the others tumbling down after it. Jethro didn't have time to throw his cutlass; his feet were already stumbling over the barrels which sent him flying across the deck in one direction, his cutlass in another.

Emoria raced across the deck and grabbed hold of the cutlass just as Jethro let out a cry. She sliced through a rope that was bound around the mast, releasing the sail that flapped in the wind, setting it free. Jethro could only hold his arms up to protect himself when the sail plummeted on top of him, swamping him with white canvas so big and so heavy he was a prisoner in seconds.

"You didn't see that coming, now did you?" chuckled Emoria. She looked at Otto. "Up you go, go fetch that parrot."

"No, I won't," said Otto.

Emoria's goggles whirred. The golden lizard poked its head out of her pocket. High at the top of the mast the monkey chattered.

"Oh I think you will," said Emoria, pointing the musket at Otto.

Otto's leg's trembled. The parrot was all he had to prove Florence's innocence.

A muffled bellow came from beneath the sail as the pirate fought his way out.

"Now!" cried Emoria, grabbing hold of Otto's arm, shaking him.

"Leave him alone," shouted Florence. "I'll get it." Florence started climbing the mast.

"Why do you want it?" asked Otto, watching Florence shinnying up the mast as nimbly as the monkey.

Emoria scooped the golden lizard out of her pocket and held it up. The mechanical creature blinked its glass eyes and flicked out its tongue.

"Isn't it beautiful, so meticulously designed. Each cog is perfectly aligned to make its movements mimic the real thing but it can't think, not like the parrot. Natisha had a gift, a secret she shared only with her brother. I see the monkey has that spark too."

Florence had reached the top of the mast and with the parrot tucked firmly under her arm she began to clamber down. Otto's mind was still whirring, like the lizard's cogs.

"That wasn't so difficult now was it?"

Emoria snatched the parrot the second Florence's feet touched the deck. She squeezed the squawking parrot inside her coat and buttoned it in, pulling tight the thick belt around her middle. The lizard crawled up her leg and slithered back inside her pocket. Emoria looked up at the monkey that still sat in the crow's nest, clapping its hands, pulling its mouth into a grin.

"I'll be watching out for you," shouted Emoria.

She pointed the musket back at Florence and Otto. "Don't you worry about Jethro, the Brigade will be only too happy to have found the thief."

"But..." started Otto. He heard the trundle of wheels on wet cobbles. He looked over the side of the galleon and saw the Brigade's steam carriage heading towards them, silhouetted by the moon. When he looked back, Emoria was gone.

As the Brigade streamed aboard the galleon, blowing their whistles, only the monkey watched Emoria Cogwright climb aboard the Golden Serpent with the sixth parrot stuffed inside her coat.

Chapter 14 – The Thief

The grunts of Jethro Silver grew louder as he thrashed his way out from beneath the sail. His head appeared between the folds, his mouth gulping mouthfuls of fresh air. Behind them footsteps pounded along the deck.

"Who called the Brigade?" asked Florence, turning to look over her shoulder at the group of men all dressed in black who were emerging out of the shadows, their capes flapping like a mighty swarm of giant bats.

It all happened so fast, Otto stood in a daze. The Brigade, their whistles blaring, were nearly upon them when finally Jethro scrambled free from the sail. There was nowhere to run. Otto's heart pounded faster. The monkey tightened its grip.

"Sold me out to the Brigade did you?" spat Jethro Silver. "Thought you'd have that reward?" Two of the pirate's teeth were missing and a gold tooth glinted right at the front.

"I... We... Didn't..." stammered Otto.

"Emoria, that figures."

"You stole the parrots," accused Florence.

"She was trying to help us," said Otto, desperately trying to think of a way off the galleon.

"She's your thief," laughed Jethro, his one eye fixed on Otto as if he were trying to take in every detail of him.

"Seize them!" came the call.

Otto felt a hand grip his shoulder so hard that he nearly toppled over with fright.

The monkey screeched.

"Get off me!" yelled Florence.

Otto watched helplessly as two guards hauled Florence, one arm each. They dragged her poor legs along the deck behind them.

"You blundering idiots, the thief is getting away," bellowed Jethro Silver, himself overpowered by the guards, his hands soon tightly bound behind his back in chains.

The guard holding Otto's arm whispered in his ear. His hot breath reeked of peppermint. "Your uncle's been looking for you, boy. You stole his monkey."

"I didn't... I..."

Otto desperately looked around him. The monkey, clamped beneath the arm of a guard, shrieked loudly. The guards marched Jethro along the deck and onto the gangplank that led back down to the harbour.

"Where are the other parrots?" called Otto, over his shoulder to the pirate.

"No talking to the prisoner boy, you're in enough trouble. I've never seen your uncle so angry."

"There were six parrots," cut in Otto, trying to get the pirate's attention.

"I only took what belonged to me," yelled back Jethro, his chains clanking just like the wind in the rigging. His legs were shackled together and all he could do was shuffle. "It's Emoria Cogwright you should be arresting, not me."

"Keep your pleas for the court, Jethro, and don't expect any leniency. Stealing mechanical parrots is nothing compared to high treason at sea. We'll see you hang for sure."

The guards roared with laughter. "We have ourselves a notorious pirate and he's trying to pass the blame."

"Your thief's getting away!" bellowed Jethro. "She planned this, tipped you off for sure. She's too clever for you."

The Brigade's steam carriage waited beside the harbour wall with Florence already huddled inside. The sound of sails straining in the wind made Otto look up, out across the harbour wall, across the swell of the black sea. A steamship cut across the water, its funnel belching smoke, its mighty sail a flash of white as bright as the moon. The name Golden Serpent was emblazoned across her helm.

Otto was pushed into the back of the steam carriage. Florence sat just inches away, a guard squashed between them whilst the rest sat up front. A second steam carriage screeched to a halt beside them. Otto watched Jethro Silver get bundled inside.

The monkey, a rope tied around its neck, was wedged on the guard's lap beside Otto. He reached out and stroked the monkey's head. He remembered what Emoria Cogwright had said. The monkey looked at Otto, his glass eyes most definitely gazing right at him. Otto wondered what Emoria had meant about the spark, puzzled over what she'd said about his mother. Otto dreaded what his uncle would say. How could Otto ask him anything about his mother now?

The steam carriage rushed through the streets, lit only by gas lamps, which cast a sickly tinge across the wet cobbles. Florence faced away from Otto, watching the terrace houses whip past. Otto was about to say something to Florence when the steam carriage jolted to a stop outside a huge soot-blackened building. It had row upon row of tiny windows and menacing brick arches. A guard flung open the carriage door and hauled Florence outside.

"Leave her alone," called Otto. "Where are you taking her?"

Florence flashed Otto a reassuring look and flicked her hair out of her face. An imposing door creaked open and Florence was swallowed inside. The steam carriage surged forward.

"Florence!" called Otto, looking back through the carriage window but Florence was gone.

"The workhouse is overrun with street urchins like her, they're like vermin. It's too good for the likes of her."

Minutes later the steam carriage pulled up outside the orangery. The front door of the house was already open wide, spilling orange light out into the street. Otto's uncle stood framed in the doorway. Delderfield Macauley's fingers were tucked into the pockets of his waistcoat. His foot tapped the front step impatiently. Otto's stomach lurched. He'd never seen his uncle look so grey. Even his moustache had lost its spring.

Otto let his uncle lead him into the house to the bottom of the wooden staircase in the entrance hall.

"You will go to your room, Otto, and there you will stay. Don't think I won't lock you in if I have to."

"But uncle... It wasn't Florence, it was the pirate and..."

"I'm not listening. You betrayed my trust and now look at what you've done."

"I didn't do anything... I..."

"Those parrots may have been just mechanical birds to you but they were so much more and now they are gone."

"I..."

"Silence!" Otto's uncle put his finger to his lips. "It's dangerous outside. I tried to protect you, gave you everything and look what you've done in return. Never again."

His uncle ushered Otto up the stairs, past the mechanical lovebirds that nestled together on a shelf and along the landing. The bottle green rug led all the way to the door of Otto's room which was guarded by a tawny owl that sat above the door. The owl's glass eyes followed every step he took. Its wings of burnished copper glowed bright in the light of the oil lamp that flickered on the wall.

"My mother designed those parrots, didn't she?"

His uncle flung open the door.

"Who told you that?"

Otto didn't like the tone of his uncle's voice or the way he shifted his gaze away.

"Why would Jethro Silver say the parrot was his?"

A flash of panic sprang into his uncle's eyes and his hand shook on the door knob.

"Don't mention that name in this house."

His uncle slammed the door shut in Otto's face.

That night Otto lay awake in bed, the picture of his mother lain upon his pillow. He wished he could remember her but all that remained of her memory were snatches of her voice, so soft, and her hair, a tumble of curls around her cheeks. As he fell into a turbulent sleep, he felt the lull of the waves and smelt the salt of the sea. He saw the locket just like his mother's but when he reached out to grab it a pirate's laughter shattered his dream.

Chapter 15 – The Box

When Otto woke, his room was still heavy with shadow. He rolled out of bed and opened the shutters. His window faced the small patch of yard at the back of the house, which was surrounded by a wall. All he could see beyond was the sky of threatening purple. Already a few spatters of rain pelted the glass. His stomach rumbled terribly but he couldn't face his uncle, not yet. He was surprised to see his door stood open just a little and there on his rug lay the monkey, curled up on its side, its eyes closed tight. Otto scooped him up.

Back on his bed, Otto turned the little brass key in the monkey's back until the monkey's eyes opened and it began to chatter.

"So you're more than just mechanical, are you?" said Otto looking closely at the monkey. "You look like a toy to me."

The monkey sprang from Otto's lap, grabbed hold of a tuft of Otto's hair and tugged it sharply.

"Ouch! Don't do that."

The monkey laughed. It sat grooming for a few seconds then it spotted something. It scampered up the bed and onto Otto's pillow.

"Don't touch it," cried Otto, only he was too late. The monkey held the photo of Otto's mother in his hands.

"Give it back."

The monkey pointed to the locket that hung around her neck and chattered loudly.

"So I didn't imagine it. You saw it too."

Otto took back the picture and tucked it away safely in a drawer beside his bed. His uncle had barely mentioned Otto's mother in all the years they had worked together, filling the orangery with trees and mechanical animals. Natisha Macauley. She had melted away with all his other memories until yesterday, when Emoria Cogwright said her name, and Jethro Silver was wearing his mother's locket.

Otto remembered in horror the tales Florence had told of the infamous steam pirate, Jethro Silver. With a sense of dread he recalled Emoria's words. Otto's uncle had never told him how his mother had come to die so young but Otto was sure the pirate knew something.

The next morning, the smell of crispy bacon and sweet porridge drew Otto downstairs. He peered around the door of the front parlour. His uncle sat at a large mahogany table, covered with a thick velvet table cloth, his head in a newspaper amidst a swirl of cherry tobacco from his pipe. Otto took his seat. A soft-cooked speckled egg, still warm, sat in a blue patterned china egg cup in his place.

"Eat whilst it's still hot," muttered his uncle, without lowering the paper.

A headline on the front page caught Otto's eye and he dropped his spoon with a clatter.

Steam Pirate to Hang

After a theft at the residential property of entrepreneur, Delderfield Macauley, the steam pirate, known as Jethro Silver, has been arrested and is held in custody. He was wanted for high treason and kidnap. He is expected to hang at noon.

The yolk on Otto's egg dribbled down the outside of the shell. The very thought of eating it made Otto's stomach curdle.

His uncle folded the newspaper and laid it on the table. There were dark bags under his eyes as if he hadn't slept a wink and his left eye had developed a twitch.

"I have to go out this morning, Otto, and as I am clearly no longer able to trust you I shall be leaving you plenty to do. The cloud machine needs a deep clean and all the plants need watering. If you finish that then there is a stack of muddy pots to scrub."

"Yes Uncle," said Otto, toying with a piece of over browned bacon. There was so much Otto wanted to ask but the coldness in his uncle's eyes stopped him.

"You'll find the broken glass in the orangery has been replaced and the potting room window fixed. I've had locks fitted to all the downstairs windows and I have the key." He patted his breast pocket.

Otto thought of Florence and his heart sank.

"I've done the very best for you Otto, more than any uncle would feel obliged to do but I simply will not have you disobey me like this." He pushed away his untouched porridge bowl, making it slop over the table.

"You let a thief break into my home."

His uncle's voice wavered and he clutched the table. His face took on a nasty red bloom.

"Then you board a pirate ship where you could have been killed."

His uncle pushed back his chair with such force that it toppled over.

"They can't hang him," said Otto. "He didn't steal your parrots, it was..."

"Enough of this," spluttered his uncle. Spit glistened in his moustache. "Don't meddle in things you don't understand."

"But..."

His uncle stormed out of the room, leaving the chair where it had fallen. A few minutes later Otto heard the front door slam shut and a key turn in the lock. He may as well be a prisoner, thought Otto.

The monkey scampered in through the doorway and ran along the wooden dresser that stood along one wall beneath an ornate gilded mirror. The monkey clutched something in its hand.

"What you got there?" called Otto, abandoning his breakfast.

The monkey screeched and leapt down from the dresser. It ran along the parlour floor and out through the door. Otto gave chase.

He followed the monkey up the stairs and along the bottle green rug until he reached his uncle's study. The monkey pushed open the door and scooted inside.

"You can't go in there," called Otto. He'd never been inside, he wouldn't have dared. His uncle had made it very clear he wasn't welcome. Otto had always wondered what his uncle did in there for hours each evening after supper. Now the monkey sat in the middle of the floor chattering excitedly. In its hand was a small brass key.

Otto squatted down beside the monkey and gently took the key away. Three of the walls were covered in shelves with books piled upon books. In addition to books, broken and incomplete mechanical animals sprawled on their backs, some with limbs missing. Some were just skeletons with no eyes at all. One wall was papered with drawings, meticulous designs of animals from every angle. Each cog and screw were detailed, like blueprints. Otto recognised the flamingos and the toucan. There were a set of drawings of fish. One was a koi carp with delicate fins and an articulated body.

Underneath the drawings stood a desk and on it Otto spotted a picture in a small oval walnut frame. The face of Otto's mother smiled back at him, her hair blowing in the wind. Standing beside her was his uncle, so much younger than he was now. His mother held a parrot, just like the ones that had been stolen.

The monkey jumped up onto the desk and pointed to a large metal box that stood beside the picture. It was a plain black box but it shook as if something inside it was alive. There was a tiny brass lock on the front, small enough for the key to fit.

"You shouldn't have stolen this," said Otto. His hand shook as he inserted the key in the lock. The monkey curled its tail around its body. Otto couldn't help thinking the monkey looked rather smug.

Otto turned the key and opened the lid. Inside a purple gelatinous blob shivered and squirmed. It was beating just like a heart. Otto caught his breath. The monkey grinned.

"I don't understand." Otto sank into his uncle's chair. "What is it?"

The monkey crept over to where Otto sat and took his hand. It placed Otto's hand on its chest amidst the coarse white fur which covered its metal skeleton. The monkey's metal fingers felt cold on Otto's. He couldn't feel anything so he pressed his ear against the monkey's chest. Sure enough, in the silence broken only by the ticking of his uncle's clock, Otto heard it. A soft hum deep inside, barely audible unless you were looking for it.

"You have a heart," exclaimed Otto.

The monkey smiled.

Chapter 16 – The Pirate Shall Hang

The monkey sat up straight, its head on one side, listening to something. Otto heard it too, a pattering sound. The monkey ran over to the window, framed by heavy drapes and peered outside. Otto joined him. He thought he saw someone, just the top of a head, but then it was gone. Florence.

Otto ran out of his uncle's study and along the hall to his own room. He peered out of the window above his bed. Nothing. The monkey opened the window catch and poked its head outside letting in a blast of cold air. There was that sound again, only louder this time. Now he could tell the sound was pebbles against glass.

"Florence," called Otto, leaning his head out of the window. "Is that you?"

Otto's face was soon wet with drizzle and he was about to give up when the monkey shrieked. There was Florence. He could just see her round the side of the house picking up pebbles from the ground.

"Flo! Florence!" shouted Otto.

Florence looked up and her face broke into a smile.

"How did you get out?" called Otto.

"Easy, no one can keep me in for long. Come on down here, there are crowds gathering in the square. They're building the gallows."

Otto thought of Jethro Silver and the headline in his uncle's newspaper.

"I can't get out," called Otto. "Uncle locked me in."

"Course you can," laughed Florence. "Haven't I taught you anything yet? Climb down."

It was a long way down and Otto felt dizzy just looking.

"They're gonna hang him," called Florence. "You should have seen the other kids' faces when I told 'em we'd been chased by cut throat Jethro Silver. The whole town will be watching him swing."

Helplessly Otto looked to the ground below. They couldn't hang the pirate, they just couldn't. Jethro knew something about his mother, he was sure of it.

"Grab your bed sheets and tie them into a rope. I'll catch you if you fall."

The monkey jumped onto Otto's bed and began tugging at the eiderdown. Otto yanked the top sheet free, then grabbed the one below. He twisted them into a rope of sorts and tied one end to the brass knob of his bedstead. He threw the other end out of the window. The monkey clambered down the sheets with ease and leapt safely to the ground by Florence's feet.

"You next," called Florence.

Otto heaved himself onto the windowsill, turned around and began to shin down the sheets. His uncle would be furious, but Otto was in so much trouble already that he just kept going. A sway of the rope made his heart miss a beat but at last his feet touched the ground. Florence slapped him on the back.

"Maybe I should be a pirate," laughed Florence, pretending to slash the air with a cutlass. "You should see the crowds. I ain't ever seen so many trying to catch a sight of someone in the courthouse. The Brigade can't hold them back."

"But he isn't the thief," said Otto. "Not really. What about Emoria Cogwright?"

"She's gone ain't she. Nowt we can do about that."

"But she's got Uncle's parrots and..."

Otto wanted to tell Florence about the locket that Jethro Silver wore around his neck, about the parrot and what he'd found in the box, but Florence was too busy play fighting with an imaginary cutlass.

They started walking. Wet washing strewn across the street between the houses hung limp and grey.

"They can't hang him," repeated Otto, kicking a pebble along the cobbles. It skipped up onto the pavement and landed in a puddle.

"That's what they do to thieves and murderers."

"But..."

"Don't tell me you feel sorry for him?"

"No... It's just..."

"Bet your uncle was in the courthouse."

"Hanging Jethro Silver won't bring back his parrots and..."

Florence stopped and held Otto's shoulder. "Spit it out."

"Jethro Silver had a locket around his neck. It looked just like my mother's."

"What of it? He's a thief."

Otto kicked another pebble, harder this time. "I need to talk to him. Both Jethro Silver and Emoria Cogwright know something about my mother and I... I can't really remember her at all."

Otto swiped away a tear from his cheek and carried on walking.

"Wait up," called Florence, running to catch up. "I get it, I do. I never knew my mam either. She died, see, when I was born. I have no family, just the other kids. We look out for each other."

"Now I'll never know," said Otto stuffing his hands deep into his pockets.

A group of children ran ahead of them and Otto could hear shouting up ahead. They'd been walking away from the harbour, down streets that all looked the same. Row after row of terraces each as grey as the next. Their doors stood open onto the street and women and children spilled outside. Otto and Florence fell in with the growing crowd.

"Where's everyone going?" called Otto over the noise of the laughter and chattering that echoed down the street. People were pushing and shoving and he was worried he'd lose sight of Florence.

"To the square, they're hanging him there at noon. No-one wants to miss it. It ain't often you see a steam pirate, let along see one swing."

Otto wondered if his uncle was in the crowd somewhere but even if he was, the street was so packed he'd never notice Otto. He followed Florence.

"Get outta the way!" cried a voice behind him. Hooves clip-clopped on the cobbles and Otto stumbled as a horse pushed its way through the crowd. The horse's flank was hot with sweat and its breath hung in the air as it pulled a wooden cart behind it laden with barrels. The cartwheels splashed through the puddles, soaking Otto's trousers. He lost sight of Florence and though he desperately searched the sea of faces, Otto couldn't see her anywhere.

Otto had all but forgotten about the monkey until he felt a soft touch on his ankle. The monkey crawled up Otto's leg and onto his shoulder and hugged its tail tightly around Otto's neck. The monkey's face touched his and Otto's tears soaked into the monkey's fur. For as long as he could remember, he'd barely thought about his mother, but she was now all he could think about. Natisha Macauley. If what Emoria Cogwright said was true, then his mother created those parrots, created everything. Maybe even the monkey with the beating purple heart. If the pirate did hang, maybe Otto would never understand.

The monkey lifted its head and started pointing. Otto looked up. Florence was jumping in the air, waving frantically in Otto's direction.

"Otto!" she called above the hubbub.

Otto pushed forward until at last he was standing beside Florence.

"There you are... I thought I'd lost you."

Otto shrugged his shoulders. He couldn't hide the smudge of tears on his cheek.

"Cheer up," said Florence. "You know what's better than watching a notorious pirate hang?"

Otto shook his head.

"Saving one of course," laughed Florence. She grabbed hold of Otto's arm and pulled him along. "I hope you know what you're doing."

Only the monkey saw Otto's uncle, walking against the tide, heading back towards the orangery.

Chapter 17 – The Plan

Otto and Florence darted through the crowd that surged like an incoming tide towards the town square.

"Down here," called Florence, dipping out of the crush and down a small alleyway that ran between two tall grey houses. The monkey ran after them, its metal hands and feet clattering along the cobbles.

"First, we've got to break into the workhouse."

"Wait for me," panted Otto. His legs were burning and his face was glowing red.

"Sitting around in that glass house has made you slow," laughed Florence.

Three streets later, Florence stopped in front of the same austere building that only yesterday the Brigade had taken him to. The workhouse. Otto struggled to catch his breath.

"Round the back," called Florence. She ran along the length of the building and squeezed into a narrow passageway between the end wall and a set of tall iron railings.

Otto followed. The passageway was only just wide enough for a child. It smelt of wet stone and ponged like chamber pots. Otto held his breath. Halfway along, Florence stood waiting. The building, four stories of blackened brick, rose up before them. Beneath a brick arch sat a tiny window. Its glass was broken, leaving a hole just big enough to wriggle through.

"Wait here," said Florence. She pulled herself up onto the window ledge and squeezed inside.

The monkey jumped up after him and peered in, swinging its tail from side to side. As the minutes passed, the thrill of saving a pirate began to seep away. Otto thought of the crowds and the Brigade and standing there in the cold drizzle, it suddenly seemed impossible.

A window opened above Otto's head and down fell a rope.

"Outa the way," came a girl's voice.

Otto looked up.

"I'm coming down."

A girl with chestnut bunches leaned out of the window. It was the same girl that Otto had spoken to that day in the harbour.

Otto shuffled along the passageway to make room as the girl came hurtling down the rope. She was closely followed by two boys, one with a shock of blond hair hung over his eyes and one as wide as he was tall with spiky black hair. Florence followed them so fast she nearly flattened them both.

"We've got a rescue party," she laughed. "This is Ginger, Spud and Blinker."

Ginger reached out to stroke the monkey but it dodged her hand and clambered up onto Otto's shoulder.

"What's this about saving a pirate?" laughed one of the boys. He swept his blond hair out of his eyes. "He'd cut your throat as soon as thank you."

Otto didn't know where to start.

"Let's just say we need him alive, Blinker," said Florence. She ushered Otto and the monkey back down the passageway the way they'd come.

"What about the Brigade?" asked the second boy, pushing up behind Otto, his breath hot against the back of Otto's neck.

"That's where you come in, Spud. You, Blinker and Ginger. You love giving the Brigade the run-around, so who better?"

"So, if we distract the Brigade for you, how are you gonna get that pirate out of chains and off the gallows?" asked Ginger as they all bundled out of the passage and back to the street outside the workhouse.

The monkey chattered excitedly.

"The monkey can get the key, I know he can," said Otto.

Ginger burst into giggles.

"Who's your new friend Florence? No toy monkey can do that," laughed Spud.

Blinkers sniggered.

Otto blushed and the monkey bared its porcelain teeth.

"This is Otto, and his uncle is none other than Delderfield Macauley. He's been hiding Otto here away in that fancy glasshouse of his, building mechanical animals. Reckon that monkey's got more brains than you, Spud. Just you wait and see."

"You won't get anywhere near that pirate," said Spud, thumping Florence on the arm. "Not even you."

"We'll see about that. We just need a horse and cart and I know where to find one of those."

Otto remembered the cart that had nearly run him over in the crowd.

"Old Mr Blenkinsop runs his errands every day, makes him so thirsty he just has to nip into the Black Horse Tavern for a drink or two. Hanging or no hanging I reckon. Me and Otto here will take care of that, you just keep the Brigade busy and keep them busy for as long as you can."

And so the plan was set, if you could call it that. Otto's heart was racing even before he chased after Florence in the direction of the Black Horse Tavern. Ginger threw Otto a beaming smile as she chased after Spud and Blinker, her red bunches swinging.

The last of the crowds walked past the Black Horse Tavern. It had stopped raining and a slant of weak sunlight fell across the tavern's sign. The air had taken on a new smell, one of anticipation. Otto could feel it too. He saw it in the faces of the people in the streets. Their voices held an edge of excitement.

"There it is," whispered Florence, pointing to the wooden cart, its horse tied up to a lamppost outside the tavern. The horse stood drinking from a tin bucket. "You jump in the back and I'll take the reins. Hang on mind, it's going to be fast."

In the distance a clock began to chime. Before it had a chance to chime twelve, Florence had leapt into the cart and grabbed hold of the reins, pulling the disgruntled horse's head out of the bucket. Otto threw himself into the back of the cart and steadied himself as the cart jolted forwards.

"We don't have long," cried Florence, driving the cart out along the street. She forced her way through a straggle of people still hurrying towards the square.

"What the... Come back here!" came a voice. It was soon joined by another and then another.

"Thief!"

"Stop them!"

But already, Florence charged past the harbour and down a street along which people were now running.

"The town square is just round the corner," called Florence as she gripped the reins even tighter.

The horse flared its nostrils and neighed indignantly. Florence pushed the poor old thing harder and faster.

The sound of a hand bell rang out and a deep voice bellowed. "Make way for the prisoner! Stand back!"

Even though the monkey clung to the side of the cart, it bounced up and down alarmingly.

"When we get to the gallows it's going to get rough," called Florence. "They'll try to stop us but Ginger, Spud and Blinker should be in place by now. Do what I say and get that monkey ready. We have only one shot at this."

"You heard him," said Otto, pulling the monkey to face him. "We need the key from the guard and we need to get Jethro Silver into the cart. Do you understand?"

The monkey screeched and clapped its hands. Otto turned the key in the monkey's back. There could be no mistakes. If this monkey really was so special, now was its chance to prove it.

Chapter 18 – The Gallows

In the centre of the town square, a wooden platform had been erected and upon it stood the gallows. A single rope hung from it, the noose carefully coiled.

Beside the noose stood the executioner with a bald head and a bushy grey beard. Dressed all in black with tall boots, his rotund middle was squeezed with a wide leather belt upon which hung a metal ring holding one iron key.

A cart stood beside the platform, pulled by a pair of black horses, their eyes blinkered by shades, their coats shiny with sweat. Inside stood the hulk of Jethro Silver flanked by two guards that barely came up to his shoulders. The steam pirate's hands were shackled behind his back in chains.

As they entered the square, Florence slowed the horse to a trot behind the gathered crowd. Otto saw a flash of red hair as Ginger raced into the crowd, then missiles started flying thick and fast. They pelted towards the Brigade who had formed a tight circle around the platform. Otto spotted Blinker and Spud throwing rotten potatoes, one after another, from a sack beside them. The potatoes smashed into the side of the platform and one hit a guard so hard it knocked his hat clean off. Spud and Blinker threw harder and faster.

"Come on, Ginger," mouthed Florence.

"Get back everyone!" yelled the guards but already the Brigade were scattered amongst the crowd.

Ginger got so close a guard almost grabbed her bunches, but she stamped on his foot and ran into the crowd letting him chase her as she weaved in and out laughing. Spud and Blinker ran in different directions drawing the guards further away from the platform.

"Come back here!" yelled the guards.

"Now!" called Florence, slapping the side of the horse.

The crowd jeered and hollered and at first they didn't notice Florence driving the horse and cart up behind them. But the executioner saw them. Jethro Silver had already stepped out of the executioner's cart and up onto the platform, and he saw Florence and Otto a second before the guards that were holding him had time to react. He kicked each guard hard, knocking them over like nine pins.

Florence drove straight through the crowd. People screamed and jumped out of the way as the horse and cart ploughed through them. Fear rose in Otto's throat like bile. They were just inches from the platform and the gallows when the monkey leapt from the cart, leapfrogging a woman's head. With another leap, the monkey landed on the platform by the executioner's feet. Otto watched the monkey scramble up the executioner's leg, grab the terrified man around the neck, and then wrap its furry arms and legs around his face. The executioner spun wildly in a crazy dance, trying to shake the monkey off.

Jethro Silver looked straight at Otto. A sparkle gleamed in his eye as he jumped off the platform and landed with a thud in the cart, nearly knocking Otto over.

"The key," called Otto, trying not to look into the face of the steam pirate who now stood so close Otto could smell stale rum on his breath. The pendant glinted around the pirate's neck.

The monkey shrieked and ran back down the executioner's front, deftly relieving him of the key from his belt. With the key grasped safely in its hand, the monkey launched into the air. Otto held his breath. The monkey sailed towards them. Otto swiped the monkey out of the air and held it aloft laughing. Florence pulled on the reins.

"Giddy up!" she cried.

Florence drove the cart out of the square, laughing with every spin of the cart's wheels. Otto couldn't believe they'd done it.

"You two should join my crew," roared Jethro Silver. "More initiative than any sailor I've ever met." He spat over the side of the cart. "But no one saves a steam pirate without wanting something in return."

Otto couldn't say a word; he was still shaking. They'd saved the steam pirate. If he wasn't standing right beside him he wouldn't have believed it. Otto heard the shrill of the Brigade's whistles. The guards gave chase, but they had no chance of catching the horse and cart on foot as it galloped out of the square and down the narrow streets.

Only the monkey saw the grey lorry with the words Hodges and Sons painted on one side, as it turned the corner heading in the direction of the orangery. Otto was too busy unlocking the padlock that held Jethro in chains and Florence was punching the air in triumph.

Chapter 19 – And Then He Was Gone

Jethro Silver shook off the chains and squatted down beside Otto.

"You've got guts, kid, but it's time I was going."

Otto stared into the face of Jethro Silver. He still couldn't quite believe he was actually sitting next to an infamous steam pirate. The words Otto wanted to say refused to come out.

"Well, ask him," called Florence, driving the cart down a narrow street they'd driven down before.

Otto was sure they must have been driving round in circles for ages, heading first left and then right down streets which all looked the same. Otto had long since lost his sense of bearings. He could no longer hear the whistles of the Brigade or the call of the gulls in the harbour. He wondered what had happened to Ginger, Spud and Blinker. And why had the Brigade just disappeared?

"Where did you get that pendant?" asked Otto at last, his words so softly spoken he hardly heard them himself.

Jethro Silver picked his teeth then leaned in close to Otto, so close that Otto could see hairs sprouting on the steam pirate's leathery chin and the pucker of the scar where once his other eye had been. The pendant hung from Jethro's neck, hypnotically swaying with the motion of the cart.

"You saved me from the hangman's noose to ask me that?"

All the questions in Otto's head began to tumble out.

"Why did you steal the parrot...? Who is Emoria Cogwright...? How does she know my mother...? Do you...?"

The steam pirate roared with laughter. "First you can't speak and now it's a barrage of questions. Well, I'd love to help but in case you've forgotten, the Brigade want me dead and riding around the streets with you will only take me back to the gallows."

Jethro Silver stood up.

"Hey!" called Florence turning round. "We just saved you from the noose. The least you could do is help us. We need the parrots and I'm sure you know something about that."

Florence pulled the cart up outside a row of terraces. "I have somewhere safe. We should lay low until dark."

"You're smart for a kid, maybe I will." The steam pirate jumped out of the cart. He reached out a hand to help Otto but the monkey let out a screech.

"Keep that thing quiet," snapped Jethro Silver.

"Follow me," said Florence, leading the way down a series of dank passageways until they stood round the back of a blackened brick terrace beneath a broken window, and Otto realised they were back at Florence's hide out.

Minutes later Otto huddled in the corner of the attic room. Florence curled up on her blanket with her notebook and charcoal. Jethro Silver looked out of the window over the street below. A wanted poster nailed to the lamppost flapped in tatters in the wind.

"You're a smart kid to have a hide-out but I ain't hanging around here long waiting for the Brigade to find me, which they will, eventually. Reckon I've outstayed my welcome in Brummington."

"That pendant..." began Otto.

"Look kid, I'm a pirate, and when a pirate sees something they like, they take it. Pendants, gold, ships, you name it. I've taken it, if I can. The Pantatlantic ocean is a dangerous place. I've lost things too."

Otto stared up at Jethro, at the jagged scar across his face.

"You took the parrot and you know Emoria Cogwright."

"Emoria and I go way back, a bigger thief you'll never find. So I wanted some of what she took, so what? What's it to you?"

"They were my uncle's and he thought Florence stole them and I had to..."

"Well they're gone now and there's nothing you or Florence over there can do about it."

Jethro snatched the notebook out of Florence's hand.

"Give that back," yelled Florence.

"That's me. Hey, that's good. They should have you drawing the wanted posters." He tossed the notebook back to Florence.

"Do you know where Emoria would take them?" Otto couldn't face his uncle, not now. He'd be furious. Otto was even more frightened of his uncle's reaction than the steam pirate at that moment.

"You don't give up, do you kid? Either of you. Well I'll be darned, you've got more pluck than most of the so-called sailors in the Black Horse Tavern. But I'll tell you this, the place Emoria Cogwright will have taken those parrots is not somewhere you would want to go."

Otto hugged the monkey tightly. The afternoon light was fading and shadows crept through the attic like a chill making Otto shiver. Jethro Silver crouched down beside him.

"Now what really made you snatch me from the gallows?"

"I thought you might know my mother," said Otto.

For a moment, Jethro Silver fell silent. He strode over to the attic window. "Well I don't." He gazed out as the afternoon gave way to evening. Otto must have nodded off. The sound of feet running up the stairs woke him. The steam pirate spun round and went for his cutlass before realising it was no longer there. The door to the attic room swung open and in burst Ginger closely followed by Spud and Blinker.

"You took your time," said Florence, tucking her notebook back inside her dress.

Their smiles fell when they saw Jethro Silver looming above them.

"Your partners in crime, I assume," he laughed.

Blinker went pale at the sight of the steam pirate and Ginger clung onto Blinker's arm.

"Don't look like that. I won't eat you."

"What happened?" said Florence. "I thought they'd caught you."

"Us? No way," said Spud. "We're the best. We gave them the run around for a while but then the Brigade were called out to that glasshouse across town. Went there in such a hurry they did. There's been a break-in."

"Delderfield Macauley's been kidnapped," butted in Blinker.

"Whoever took him made a right mess of the place," piped up Ginger.

"But why would anyone…?" At that moment, Otto crumpled.

The monkey shrieked.

"Looks like Emoria Cogwright decided to come back for the rest," said Jethro Silver.

Otto thought of the black metal box and the beating purple mass within and his heart sunk.

Chapter 20 – A Pirate's Promise

"But why would Emoria take my uncle?" Otto muttered from the floor.

The monkey snuggled up to Otto's neck and made soothing clicking sounds. All the bounce had been expelled from Florence.

"What will you do?" she asked, but Otto just shook his head.

Jethro Silver paced the room. The floorboards creaked with every circuit. Ginger, Spud and Blinker slipped quietly away. After the excitement of the rescue, Otto felt cold and empty. He had no more answers than he did the day before and now he'd helped free a notorious steam pirate -- and for what? He'd lost his uncle, the only person Otto had in the whole world. He remembered his uncle's words: *It's dangerous outside.* He hadn't wanted to listen then, and now look what had happened.

Jethro Silver stopped pacing and pulled Otto up off the floor.

"We need a plan," he said, pulling Florence up too.

"We?" said Florence. "I thought you were leaving."

"Maybe I changed my mind. You see, I don't like it when someone messes with my friend."

"Your friend?" said Otto, raising his head up to look at the steam pirate.

"You think pirates don't have friends? Do you think we just plunder and loot ships and sail the high seas? Well we do a lot of that but before I was a pirate I too had a friend."

"Who?" said Florence, listening intently now.

"Oh, I couldn't have been much older than you when I first met him. We both loved the sea and boats. How we loved boats and we planned to travel the world. But that was then. I haven't seen him for a very, very long time but he'll always be my friend."

"What's that got to do with my uncle being kidnapped?"

Then Otto remembered the photograph of two small boys that hung in the hallway of the orangery in amongst his uncle's pictures.

"Do you mean my uncle?"

"Delderfield and I were inseparable, thick as thieves, just like you two."

"Does that mean you'll help?" asked Otto.

Jethro said nothing for a few minutes. In fact, it looked like he wasn't listening to what Otto said at all.

"Will you?" repeated Otto.

"Will I what?" snapped Jethro Silver.

"Will you go after Emoria Cogwright?"

"Well it's got her grubby marks all over it," said Jethro Silver.

"We could come with you," said Florence.

"Hey, slow down. Haven't I already told you, the Pantatlantic Ocean is no place for a kid and Emoria Cogwright ain't someone you want to deal with. Things can get real bad, real quick."

"I could be your crew," said Florence. "I'm not scared of the ocean."

"My crew don't stick around for long," said Jethro. "There's a reason for that. You listen and you listen good. Never underestimate the dangers of the ocean. I'm not the only pirate, not the worst or the ugliest by a long way neither. You wouldn't even be talking with some of them, you'd already be dead."

Otto caught his breath. He remembered his nightmares and his skin began to shiver.

"You won't know unless you give me a chance," said Florence.

Otto was sure Emoria Cogwright knew things about his mother. And why would Emoria have stolen the parrots? How did she even know about them? He thought of his home being ransacked. What had been taken? Maybe there were clues.

"I'm going back home to see what happened," said Otto. "I can't stay here forever and no one will see me in the dark."

"Oh no you don't," said Jethro Silver. "And let you lead the Brigade straight back to me?"

"You can't stop me." Otto was angry, angry about everything.

Florence opened the door that led out of the attic. "I'll come with you."

Otto turned to follow.

"Wait up! You got food in that house of yours?"

Otto nodded.

"It's hungry work being rescued. Lead the way. You gotta know how to be unseen. Night time is the pirate's weapon. The shadows hide everything. I've looted a galleon before anyone has opened an eye."

And so the four of them crept through the shadows; a steam pirate, two kids, and a mechanical monkey. They darted from alleyway to alleyway and slid between houses, seen only by a black rat that sat watching them, and a dog tied up in a back yard.

The door to Delderfield Macauley's house swung open on its hinges. Dirty footprints ran the length of the tiled hall and through into the house. In the dining room, the table was set for lunch. Abandoned soup congealed in its bowl. Drawers in the sideboard sat open and cupboards had been emptied onto the floor. A terracotta pot lay smashed, the plant now a mess of broken stems in a sea of earth across the rug.

"Why did she have to do that?" gasped Otto.

"Emoria likes others to get their hands dirty," said Jethro Silver, kicking aside the smashed pot to reach the table.

Otto thought of the three delivery men who'd stolen the parrots. The monkey screeched loudly.

Jethro Silver grabbed a chunk of bread and cheese from the table. Otto ran out into the orangery, the monkey close on his heels. Clouds from the cloud machine drifted above him but the orange trees and palms were empty. Flamingos no longer waded in the babbling stream. The monkey scooped up a salmon pink tail feather that floated along its surface.

"Come and look," called Florence.

Otto ran into his uncle's workshop. Pots had been knocked over and crates of metal cogs and screws upturned onto the floor. Paint pots lay on their side oozing pink and orange paint. A mechanical snail lay crushed near where Florence stood. Otto crouched down to touch it. A tear trickled down his cheek.

"Oh Florence," he cried. "They've taken the flamingos and..."

Remembering the black metal box on his uncle's desk, Otto raced back into the hall and bounded up the stairs two steps at a time. He ran along the bottle green rug, watched by the owl above the door, just as the owl had watched the three delivery men that lunchtime. The door to his uncle's study stood wide open. Inside, Otto let out a cry.

Every drawing had been ripped from the wall and the black metal box was gone. The picture of his mother with his uncle and the parrot lay on the floor, the glass of the frame broken. Otto picked it up. When he looked up, Jethro Silver stood before him. He took the picture from Otto's hands. The broken glass had nicked Otto's finger and it oozed with blood.

"It's my mother," said Otto, sucking his finger.

"Natisha, Delderfield's sister," said Jethro, standing the picture back on Delderfield's desk. "Inventors, both of them, just like their parents. Only better, because they combined their love of nature with their gift of all things mechanical."

"So you did know my mother!" cried Otto. "You lied to me."

"Pirates are good liars," said Jethro. "Your uncle was my friend and Natisha his twin sister, though they were nothing alike. She lived for crazy creatures. Delderfield lived to travel."

"I have to find him," sniffed Otto. "And his parrots. They were so very important to him."

"We'll find him, I promise," said Jethro.

"How can I trust you? You lied to me and you're a criminal, why else would they want to hang you?"

"You can trust a pirate's promise. It's our honour. I owe your uncle."

Chapter 21 – Gostopolus Island

The monkey jumped up onto Delderfield's desk. It screeched as it paced up and down, its tail held high. Florence stood in the doorway munching a wedge of bread and cheese, clasping an apple in her other hand.

"What's wrong with him?" she asked.

"It's gone," said Otto, finding it hard to take it all in.

"What's gone?" said Florence. She took a large bite of apple and crunched noisily.

"The box," said Otto. "It was here earlier. It had something inside, something purple. Whatever it was, it beat just like a heart. I'm sure the monkey has some of it inside him. I can hear it, feel it."

"Now things are starting to make sense," said Jethro Silver.

"What do you mean?" Otto didn't trust Jethro, not just because he was a steam pirate but because he was a liar.

"It explains why Emoria Cogwright took the parrots and why she came back when she realised what she had."

The monkey screeched even louder. Florence swiped him off the desk. "Stop doing that," she cried.

Otto snatched up the monkey and hugged him tightly. The monkey was all he had left. "It's all right," he soothed, but the monkey was so agitated Otto couldn't hold him still.

"What's going on?" Florence tossed the apple core in a metal bin beside the desk. "What 'ave I missed?"

Jethro pulled the chair out from under the desk and sat down. "Natisha had a gift, unlike anything Delderfield could match." He put his feet up on the desk. "She studied chemistry, elements, compounds and formulas. She was determined to bring her mechanical animals to life. Give them emotions and thoughts of their own. That's why she and her brother argued."

Otto sat crossed legged on the floor. He tried to coax the monkey over to him as he listened to the steam pirate.

"Delderfield couldn't see her passion. He wanted to build machines and ships."

Otto pointed to the picture of his mother holding the mechanical parrot. It was almost exactly like the parrots his uncle had made and Otto had painted. "Did my uncle give his parrots a heart? Is that why Emoria Cogwright took them?"

"Emoria is a collector and not just any collector. She scours the globe looking for new mechanical creatures and she'll stop at nothing to get them. Don't be fooled by her appearance. She's calculated and ruthless." Jethro rummaged amongst a pile of rolled tubes of paper down beside the desk. "She's more dangerous than any pirate and she wouldn't have been able to resist those parrots."

"But why take Otto's uncle?" interrupted Florence.

"He's the only one who knows Natisha's secret."

"Then we steal the box back and rescue Otto's uncle," cried Florence. She pulled Otto up off the floor and flung her arm around her friend. "We'll be your crew, won't we Otto?"

Jethro pulled out a roll of paper and spread it out over the desk. It was a map.

"Look and look real good." Jethro Silver pointed to the vast blue of the Pantatlantic Ocean. Right at one end sat a tiny dot. "Gostopolus Island, that's where she's heading. Seven days at sea if the wind is behind you, if you make it that far. No one has been there and come back alive."

Something had been bothering Otto the whole time Jethro had been talking. Where was his mother now and why couldn't he remember her? It was something his uncle would never discuss and Otto had given up asking.

"Do you know what happened to my mother?" asked Otto.

"She died," said Jethro Silver. He rolled up the map. "It was a long time ago. It's unwise to ask so many questions."

Florence looked from the steam pirate to Otto. "We should go now, whilst it's still dark."

The monkey clapped its hands.

"Even the monkey agrees with me," laughed Florence.

"A promise is a promise," said Jethro Silver, getting up. "But don't go thinking it'll be easy. Worse things always happen at sea."

As the four of them left the orangery and slipped through the back streets to the harbour, three pairs of eyes were watching them. The monkey sensed their presence and chattered on Otto's shoulder, but the steam pirate resolutely led the way, oblivious. It wasn't until Otto could hear the clanging of the rigging in the wind and the lapping of the water against the harbour wall that he heard the screeching of wheels behind them.

Chapter 22 – The Ambush

A hand tugged Otto's sleeve.

"Down here," came a whisper.

Otto saw the whites of Ginger's eyes. Her bunches were moving shadows against the wall. He saw a flash of Blinker's hair.

"What the...?" gasped Jethro Silver as he too was pulled into the dark alleyway, followed seconds later by Florence.

The Brigade's steam carriage sped past and shuddered to a halt at the end of the street by the harbour wall.

"Hey, Ginger, what are you doing 'ere?" whispered Florence.

"They've been watching you, waiting for you to make a move. We saw them as we left," said Ginger.

"If you're heading for the steam galleon you'll never make it," said Spud.

"You try and stop me," hissed Jethro Silver. He peered round the corner of the alleyway out onto the cobbled street.

The steam carriage had turned around and stood facing towards them. Its headlamps turned the ever-present smog that hung over the cobbles an unnerving shade of orange.

"I'd thought they'd given up," said Otto.

The monkey curled its tail around Otto's ankle and chattered softly.

"Forget about an escaped steam pirate?" said Blinker. "No way."

"Keep your voices down," snapped Jethro Silver. "Looks like I'm going alone, three's a crowd anyway."

"No you're not," said Florence. "We're your crew, aren't we Otto?"

Otto's heart was thumping loudly in his ears. "Yes, we are," he said. "And you promised."

Jethro Silver ground his teeth and kicked the ground.

The steam carriage started moving slowly, making its way down the street to where Otto and the others hid.

"Move back," warned Florence. "They'll see us."

"Skirt round the back of the houses and double back, then take the alleyway straight through to the harbour. They won't be able to follow you. We'll head back to the workhouse for reinforcements and meet you at the corner opposite the harbour wall," said Ginger.

Spud and Blinker nodded in agreement.

"They'll see us," said Jethro Silver.

"Yeah, but there'll be loads of us by then. We'll hold them back whilst you make a run for it."

"But..." said Otto.

"That could work," interrupted Jethro Silver. "Now scram, we don't have all night."

Excitement flashed in Ginger's eyes as she turned and ran. Spud and Blinker were already running.

Florence led the way, down passageways so dark that Otto could barely see where he was going. The monkey curled around Otto's neck and chattered in his ear. At last they were nearly back to the orangery.

From there Florence darted down a narrow alleyway squashed between iron railings. It took them past the back yards of street after street of terraces and under a brick archway. Up ahead, Otto saw the sea and tasted salt on his lips.

Florence stopped. "Wait here," she called.

Ahead of them lay the harbour, and moored on the left was the hulk of the steam galleon. A crescent moon broke through the clouds above the skull and crossbones. The steam carriage crawled up and down the road alongside the harbour wall, hunting its prey. The galleon looked tantalisingly near but even Otto realised that in the time it would take them to run over to it and climb the gangplank the Brigade would be upon them like a swarm.

The seconds dragged like hours but at last Otto heard a stampede of feet heading their way.

"'Ere they come," called Florence.

"When I give the signal, you run," butted in Jethro Silver, pushing in front of Florence. "Whatever happens, keep running. No looking back until you're on board the galleon. Do you hear me?"

Otto nodded. The monkey tightened its grip around Otto's neck.

The steam carriage spotted the gang of boys and girls running helter-skelter down the cobbled street just as Ginger, Spud and Blinker led them past where Otto and the others waited. The steam pirate threw down his arm as a signal and streaked out across the road. Otto ran too with Florence beside him. They weaved through the stragglers at the back of the group. The children wielded a motley array of improvised weapons. One waved a broom and another a mop. Others brandished battered saucepans which they beat with wooden spoons.

The steam carriage raced towards them until it found itself surrounded and unable to move. Otto kept running, his eyes following the flowing locks of Jethro Silver.

The doors of the steam carriage burst open releasing the guards into the crowd of children. Their screams and shouts were joined by the shrill of the guards' whistles.

Otto saw Jethro Silver step onto the gangplank of the steam galleon, Florence close on his tail. Otto had just made it across the road when he tripped on the kerb stone and down he fell. The monkey screeched as it flew out of Otto's grasp. His knee throbbed and his twisted ankle burned with pain.

"Otto," called Florence.

Otto scrambled to his feet before he realised the monkey had gone. In a panic, Otto spun round. The monkey lay sprawled on the cobbles. Otto reached out to pick it up when a hand wrenched the back of his shirt.

"Run!" cried Florence, waving from the gangplank.

Already the galleon hissed with steam. A huge belch erupted from her engine. Otto heard the creaking of the huge galleon trying to escape the hold of its tether, like a bull straining on its leash.

Otto pulled away hard and his shirt ripped itself free. The guard snatched up the monkey and blew his whistle. The monkey screeched so loudly, Otto could hear it all the way up the gangplank.

"What kept you?" hollered Jethro Silver as he tossed the mooring rope over the side. The vast metal vessel, giant wings protruding from its belly, eased away from the harbour wall. Hurriedly Jethro Silver raised the gangplank.

"I lost the monkey," gasped Otto. "I can't leave it... I..."

"We must," snapped Jethro Silver.

Otto fought back tears. He felt the surge of the mighty galleon beneath him and the pull of the wind in her sails.

"Otto, wait!" came a cry.

Otto ran to the side of the galleon, now several feet away from its mooring. The black sea churned beneath them.

Ginger stood on the sea wall holding the monkey up above her head.

"Catch!" she cried.

Florence had already seen her. She grabbed hold of a net on a long pole from the deck and reached it out over the side of the galleon as far as she could.

"All steam ahead," bellowed Jethro Silver from the helm.

Ginger threw the monkey and Otto held his breath.

The monkey sailed across the void beneath it.

"Caught it," laughed Florence as she scooped the monkey out of the air.

The galleon picked up steam as it left the harbour. Otto hugged the monkey tightly and waved at the silhouetted figure of Ginger until he could no longer see her. The steam galleon, driven by a mighty wind, whisked them out of the port of Brummington towards the Pantatlantic ocean, headed for Gostopolus Island.

Chapter 23 – The Sound of the Sea

Otto sat on deck with Florence long into the night. The wind was behind them and the steam galleon surged out to sea. Easterly gusts blew away the clouds and by the light of the moon, Otto watched the fathoms of swirling black water beside them. He listened to the sails rustling as they billowed in the breeze, and the splashes and as the galleon cut its way through the sea. Jethro Silver never left the helm.

Salt water sprayed over Otto's face and he was lulled to sleep by the rocking of the waves but his sleep was punctuated by dreams so vivid they seemed real. He saw Jethro Silver looking down at him, only the steam pirate's face had fewer creases and two blue eyes. Jethro's mane of black curls was framed against the sun which warmed Otto's face. He heard his mother laughing and the squawk of a parrot. When he reached out for her the ship began to rock and her laughter turned to screams. His mother sounded further and further away until he could no longer hear her. Otto woke, his entire body wet with sweat. He was wrapped in a scratchy blanket. The face of Jethro Silver looked down at him, a jagged scar where once an eye had been.

"Call yourself crew?" laughed Jethro Silver, pulling aside the blanket. He slammed down a tin mug of scalding black tea. "You should have been up with the sun like Florence. Up there."

Otto shielded his eyes and looked up to the crow's nest at the top of the mast. There sat Florence, her notebook in hand, scribbling. The Pantatlantic ocean stretched out around them and the water glistened turquoise. The monkey lay beside Otto on deck, its eyes closed.

The first few days at sea saw Otto's hair become encrusted in salt and his face redden with the glare of the sun on the water. He no longer washed and had abandoned his shoes, just like Florence. His uncle would have been appalled. Otto and Florence learned how to raise the sails, scrub the deck and fish for their supper over the side of the galleon. They caught shiny silver mackerel and crabs by the dozen. Though Otto thought of his uncle and the parrots often, he couldn't stop thinking about the steam pirate.

Every night, Otto dreamed of his mother, though he never saw her face, and Jethro Silver was always there. Even when Otto wasn't sleeping he heard snatches of the steam pirate's voice in his head. The sound of the sea as it rose and fell was achingly familiar, so too the smell of the galleon and the feel of the motion of the ship as the wind blew it further and further through the Pantatlantic ocean. Otto knew he'd seen and smelt it all before, so very long ago, but he couldn't think why. They felt like stirrings of a memory he never knew he had and each day more of these images and sensations began to take shape and slide into place. These were glimpses of a life he could never have imagined having. They had nothing to do with the orangery or his uncle or the life he'd been living since he arrived in Brummington. These memories were much older.

"Florence, can you forget a life?"

Florence was picking potatoes out of the bottom of a hessian sack. She threw them into a large metal bowl. The monkey sat watching Otto who was cross-legged on deck peeling potatoes with a penknife, being careful not his nick his fingers as he scraped away the peel.

"What do you mean?" asked Florence, missing the bowl. A potato rolled across the deck. The shadow of a large cloud fell across them and goosebumps prickled on Otto's bare legs.

Otto knew something, felt it in every bone of his body, but until then, hadn't been able to put it into words. "Can you forget something, something really important, as if it never happened?"

Florence took the pile of peeled potatoes and plopped them into a large pan full of water. Jethro Silver popped his head above deck.

"Get those spuds down here, one of you."

Waves crashed against the side of the galleon and a fierce wind rocked her from side to side. Grey clouds scudded across the sky which had changed from blue to a threatening mauve.

"Yeah, you can," said Florence, spilling water that sloshed over the side of the pan as she tried to walk in a straight line across a deck that shifted beneath her.

"There's a storm brewing," bellowed Jethro Silver, going back below deck.

Florence stopped and put down the pan. "Sometimes your brain forgets things, bad things, difficult things."

"How do you know?" said Otto.

A spot of rain landed on his leg and he wiped it away.

"I didn't remember my own baby brother dying in my lap until old Mrs Grobisher's baby died two winters ago. She was the only one who cared about me in the workhouse but she left soon after."

The sky rumbled.

"She's the one who told me that sometimes it's kinder for the mind to forget. But that those memories can wake up when you least expect it."

"You said your mum died when you were born," said Otto.

"Well some memories I don't want to remember," said Florence.

Heavier rain drops began to fall, soaking into Otto's hair. Florence picked up the pan again and staggered with it to the hatch. "Why do you ask?"

"It was the sound of the sea at first," said Otto, following her. "Then I remembered Jethro Silver and I remembered a ship like this."

Chapter 24 – The Storm

"Give that to me," bellowed Jethro Silver, reaching up out of the hatch. He grabbed the heavy pan from Florence and disappeared with it to the galley below.

Florence and Otto sat in the galley on upturned wooden barrels pulled up against a small wooden table. By the time the potatoes had boiled, a storm was battering the galleon. Florence's face drained of all colour and Otto had no appetite for the potatoes that Jethro Silver heaped into a bowl.

"Get it down you, we're in for a long night ahead of us."

Tin bowls and mugs slid across the table and Otto nearly went flying when the galleon lurched to one side.

"The sea's too rough to sail," said Jethro, having demolished a bowl of potatoes and boiled onion soup. "It's time to fly."

Otto remembered the wings attached to each side of the galleon's belly, the same wings that Jethro had retracted when they sailed out of Brummington harbour.

"You'll get soaked out there so put something on."

Jethro Silver left the galley and returned with a couple of leather overcoats, brass buttons down the front and cuffs so large Otto had to turn them over four times before he could see his hands. The coat came down to just above his ankles. Florence too was swamped, and only her nose stuck out above the collar.

"Do what I say and do it quick and I'll see if I can fly us out of the eye of the storm."

The monkey sat chattering in the middle of the table.

"Keep that thing inside," yelled Jethro Silver before disappearing out of the galley and along the corridor that led up to the hatch to the deck.

"You heard him," said Otto to the monkey.

The galleon lunged to the left and the monkey slid along the table and onto the floor. There it stayed, in the corner with its hands over its head.

A blast of wind hit Otto as soon as he pushed open the hatch and clambered out on deck. Florence followed close behind.

"Over here," yelled Jethro Silver.

The steam pirate's voice now sounded very familiar and Otto desperately tried to remember what he must have forgotten but the bitter cold soon cleared his mind. He shivered uncontrollably. He and Florence forced their way against the wind across the deck to where Jethro Silver stood at the helm. The steam pirate stood in front of a complex array of switches and buttons next to the ship's wheel. Jethro Silver yanked one of a row of levers that were wet with rain.

"You two pull the second lever on the right and don't stop until you hear the wings latch into place." He had to shout and even then his words were snatched by the wind. His wet hair was plastered across his face so he could hardly speak at all.

Otto's feet slipped on the flooded deck and he struggled to keep a grip on the lever but Florence clasped her hands over Otto's. Together they pulled with all their might. When Otto thought he couldn't pull any longer and his fingers were white and numb, there was a terrific clang followed by the sound of canvas pulling taut against the wind. The galleon's wings had sprung into place.

They beat the air like the wings of a gigantic dragon. Otto felt his feet sliding. The deck reared up as the galleon launched itself out of the water with a tremendous splash and soared into the air. The thrum of her engines was deafening. Otto slipped halfway down the deck before he managed to grab hold of one of the masts. He struggled to keep himself upright.

"Hold tight!" called Jethro Silver who stood at the control panel flicking switches.

A crack of lightning erupted in the sky in a jagged scar of bright white. A clap of thunder boomed directly overhead. Jethro Silver took the wheel. His wet hair streamed out behind him as the galleon steamed across the ocean just above the surface of the raging waves. Otto's stomach lurched and he shut his eyes tight.

The galleon circled round the edge of the storm. When Otto opened his eyes again he saw a break in the cloud up ahead and a beacon of clear sky beyond. The galleon levelled out and Otto's heart returned to a steady beat.

"Nothing to worry about," called Jethro Silver. "In sailing mode the galleon takes care of herself but flying can be a bit trickier if we have to head into the wind."

Florence clung to another mast just feet away from Otto. She trembled, her face as white as the sails. Otto was so close he was sure that if he took a few steps he could reach out and touch her. Florence's eyes stared wide and her teeth chattered uncontrollably.

"I'm coming!" called Otto into the wind.

He let go of the mast just as the galleon hit a gust of wind so strong that it snatched the wheel out of Jethro Silver's hands. Otto was thrown off balance and onto the deck where he began to roll.

Otto screamed.

The galleon rose so steeply that Otto rolled faster and faster. He heard the roar of the steam pirate and the sound of feet running towards him but Otto hit the side of the galleon and was catapulted upwards.

In a blinding panic, Otto grabbed hold of the galleon's rail as his legs flew over the side. He gripped the rail tightly but his legs hung overboard. It was only the speed of the galleon that kept them suspended in the air. In the next minute, one that felt like hours, Otto desperately tried to pull himself back onboard.

A pair of strong hands grabbed hold of his. He looked up into the face of Jethro Silver.

"I've got you," shouted Jethro. "Just hang on."

Otto couldn't speak. His mouth was too dry to form words. Jethro Silver pulled him hard and Otto felt himself being dragged back over the rail which dug into his stomach. The steam pirate clenched his teeth. In the next tug, he wrenched Otto clear of the rail and in that moment Otto heard the voice of his mother calling his name. He saw her face looking over the side of the galleon, next to Jethro's. The steam pirate's two blue eyes were full of fear. Tears pricked Otto's eyes and without thinking about it he shouted.

"Father!"

With an almighty heave, Jethro hauled Otto back onboard and held him tightly.

"Thank goodness, Otto. I couldn't have lost you a second time."

Chapter 25 – Pirate Blood

The galleon steamed across the ocean until the sky bloomed pink and orange. Otto stood next to Jethro Silver at the wheel. The steam pirate had bundled Florence in a thick blanket and set her down beside them at the helm.

It still hadn't sunk in. Jethro Silver had saved his life twice now but Otto could barely recall the first time, he'd been so young. So that was why the galleon seemed so familiar, why it felt like a deep and hidden memory. It was. Like cogs clicking into place, the memories came flooding back.

Otto remembered sitting on deck with his mother. He'd played with a mechanical parrot whilst his mother had helped Jethro Silver raise the sails. But Otto still couldn't recall why they were there or why they had left. He'd dreamed of his mother screaming, night after night, and only now did he remember that it was because he'd fallen overboard.

"You saved my life, didn't you?" said Otto.

Florence cradled a mug of steaming tea and listened intently.

"You seem to make a habit of trying to fall off my ship."

"When I didn't remember you, why didn't you say something?" asked Otto. What he really wanted to know was why he'd ended up with his uncle.

Jethro Silver scanned the horizon. Night had painted the sky black and stolen the last of its warmth.

"It was a long time ago."

"But you're my father, aren't you?"

"I don't think your uncle would ever admit that and I wasn't welcome."

Otto wished he understood why everything had changed.

"What happened to my mother?"

"Some things are best forgotten. I'll set us down on the water, you two go below deck. Look after Florence, she looks like she's lost her sea legs."

There was so much Otto needed to know but it looked like the conversation was over. The steam pirate turned his back on Otto and stared back out to sea.

Down below deck, Otto and Florence lay in their small airless cabin. A pair of wooden bunks swayed with the swell of the ocean as the galleon surged onwards. Otto curled up in a tight ball under an itchy blanket.

"You're the son of a steam pirate," said Florence, propping herself up on her elbows. A warm glow had transformed her pale cheeks. "That makes you a pirate."

"No it doesn't," snapped Otto. Having a father, one you never knew you had, took some getting used to. "Maybe I don't want to be a pirate."

Otto tried to sleep but he knew he wouldn't. He heard Jethro Silver climb below deck and into the bunk next door. Florence started snoring. There were too many questions tumbling around inside Otto's head. Why wouldn't Jethro talk about his mother? Why didn't his father want him?

The galleon creaked and groaned. Shadows bounced around the wood-panelled cabin from the lantern that swung from the ceiling. It seemed his uncle had secrets too. A thought struck Otto, so hard he shot up in his bunk, dislodging the monkey that had curled up beside him. His uncle had let the Brigade take Jethro Silver, knowing full well they would send him to the gallows. How could his uncle allow his father to be hanged?

Otto's eyes began to droop as the hours slipped by, but a tapping sound kept him awake. It was coming from the deck above and it sounded like footsteps. The monkey chattered. Someone was aboard the galleon.

The hairs on Otto's arms bristled and his heart began to thump. The monkey shook Florence's shoulder.

"Florence, wake up," cried Otto.

The door to their cabin burst open.

"We've been boarded!" whispered Jethro Silver.

The light from the lantern caught the blade of a cutlass in his hand. A musket nestled in the leather holster strapped around the steam pirate's shoulder. "Stay below deck and don't make a sound."

"But... who...?" stammered Otto.

Florence sat up and patted down her hair.

"These waters are crawling with pirates looking for easy pickings."

"We're your crew," piped up Florence, straightening her glasses.

"Unless you can aim a musket or fire a cannon you're no good to me."

Before Otto could say another word, Jethro Silver was gone. Already he was climbing the ladder to the deck above. The monkey shrieked and clutched onto Otto's arm.

"We can't just stay 'ere and wait for a pirate to cut our throats," said Florence. She pulled on a leather coat that had lain crumpled in a heap at the end of the bunk. "You coming?"

Otto imagined the pirates creeping along the deck. He thought of the pirate stories that had terrified him.

"There's nothing on board to steal," said Otto.

"There's the galleon, stupid. This is no ordinary pirate ship." Florence threw the other leather coat at Otto. "Get dressed, we can't let them take it."

"What if they make us walk the plank?" shuddered Otto, struggling to get his arms into the leather coat which was still damp.

"Then we die defending it," said Florence. "I wish I had a musket."

"Jethro told us to stay below," said Otto.

The monkey chattered loudly and jumped off the bunk. It scampered after Florence.

"You've got pirate blood," called back Florence.

Otto chased after them, up the ladder. They all peeked through the hatch. Out on deck Jethro Silver shouted.

"Get off my ship before I slice you in two and feed you to the sharks!"

Otto and Florence crawled up on deck and hid behind a pile of barrels, held in place with a thick rope. Otto clamped his hand over the monkey's mouth.

"You talking to us?" laughed a pirate. He slashed a cutlass though the air. The pirate's trousers were stuffed into chunky boots, and a pair of large brass googles were clamped over his greasy black hair. He had the longest beard Otto had ever seen.

"Your crew deserted you, have they?" laughed a second pirate, who was short and skinny. Long pointy boots stuck out under a pair of purple stripey trousers. A peaked leather cap squashed his blond curls and large copper hoops pierced his ears. "Maybe they ran away," he sneered.

Florence jumped up. Otto tried to pull her back but there was no stopping her. "We're his crew," cried Florence.

Both pirates burst out laughing when they saw Florence in her oversized coat. Over the side of the galleon Otto saw a wooden pirate ship, half the size of the steam galleon. It rocked in the waves beside them. Otto caught sight of two, maybe three more pirates aboard it, though they were just shadows in the dark. Florence was going to get them all killed.

Jethro Silver stood his ground. He pulled Florence close and put his arm around her shoulder.

"The crew are sleeping," he lied. "We wouldn't want to wake them, now would we?"

The pirate with the long beard slashed his cutlass just inches from the end of Jethro's nose. Otto felt his blood drain down into his toes.

"We know who you are. Jethro Silver. And we know you have no crew. Now we'll be taking this fine vessel of yours. If you don't want to be swimming with the sharks get into that rowing boat down there, the one we've been towing."

The second pirate roared with laughter.

"At least you won't drown. You can paddle back to land, which is that way." He pointed back towards the direction of Brummington, a good four days sailing in a steam galleon across the ocean.

Something snapped inside Otto. He couldn't bear to see his father ridiculed. He remembered how easily Emoria Cogwright had outwitted Jethro. Otto looked at the monkey and the monkey nodded, as if it too had a plan.

Otto ran along behind the stack of barrels making sure he remained hidden. He slipped the rope securing the stack off of its hook, then knocked over the last barrel in the row. Once on its side, he used his legs to push really hard so that it rolled across the deck, surprising the pirates. Then, the barrel bashed into the stripey legs of the first pirate making him cry out. It was all the distraction Jethro Silver needed.

In that split second Jethro snatched the cutlass out of the pirate's hand. The monkey raced across the deck and launched itself at the second pirate, landing on his beard. The pirate screamed. Hanging on tightly, the monkey climbed the pirate's beard and then wrapped itself around the pirate's face. The pirate dropped his cutlass to the deck with a clatter and Jethro kicked it towards Florence who stooped down and grabbed it.

Jethro, Otto and Florence formed a tight circle around the two pirates. Florence held the cutlass out in from of her, gripping it in both hands just like Jethro. The blades glinted in the moonlight. The monkey crawled onto the pirate's head and clung on, clasping its metal hands over the pirate's eyes. The monkey didn't let go no matter how much the pirate danced and thrashed.

Never before had Otto felt such a rush of excitement. Maybe he really did have pirate blood. But the feeling of triumph was shattered by the sound of a cannon being fired and the crash of a cannon ball smashing into the side of the galleon, sending Otto flying.

Chapter 26 – Cannon Fire

Otto lay spread-eagled on the deck. The stench of acrid gunpowder hung in the air and made him cough. A second cannon ball struck the galleon seconds later. Otto threw his hands over his head.

"They're firing at us!" cried Florence.

Otto looked up. The two pirates hadn't moved. Jethro Silver now had his musket aimed straight at them. He called over his shoulder. "Get to the cannons, I'll hold these two."

"But how do we…?" cried Otto, picking himself up.

"Pack the cannon with gunpowder, then wadding, and load in a cannon ball. Then light the fuse," bellowed Jethro Silver. "Now run, before we get sent to the ocean floor."

Florence caught Otto's arm. Together they raced towards the hatch. The monkey ran behind them. The galleon shook with a another explosion so violent that the monkey lost its footing on the ladder and tumbled down on top of Florence.

"Down another level," shouted Florence, stuffing the monkey under her arm. He rounded a corner and disappeared down another ladder. "Grab a lantern."

Otto slipped into the cabin and unhooked the lantern. It was hot and stuffy in the bowels of the galleon. The light from the lantern flitted along the corridor and its flame flickered as if it were about to go out.

"The metal hull will hold for now," called Florence, turning into a room on their left.

Before them stood a row of cannons jutting out of shiny brass portholes. A pyramid of cannon balls stood in one corner alongside a large keg of gunpowder.

"We can't fire a cannon," said Otto.

"Oh yes we can," said Florence. "Unless you want to end up food for the sharks."

Otto thought of the jagged scar across Jethro's face and felt sick. "I can't swim."

"Why does that not surprise me?" laughed Florence. "Some pirate you are."

Florence loaded gunpowder into one of the cannons whilst the monkey held up the lantern. Then she pushed in a handful of wadding and packed it down with a long stick she'd found leaning up against the keg of gunpowder.

"Don't just stand there, help me," snapped Florence, as she struggled to carry a cannon ball.

"How do we know where we're firing?" asked Otto as together they heaved the cannon ball into the barrel of the gun.

"These cannons point north-east, exactly where the pirate ship is waiting."

"But how…?"

"You're gonna 'ave to know how to read the night sky if you're gonna be a pirate. Didn't your uncle teach you anything in that fancy glass house of yours?"

Florence struck a match. "Cover your ears, this is gonna blow."

Boom!

Otto's ears were still ringing when they re-loaded the cannon. By the third explosion the ringing was joined by the sound of splintering wood.

"We hit them!" cried Florence triumphantly, punching the air. "Bet she'll sink. Let's go and look."

Otto ran back to the hatch with Florence. The monkey darted up on deck and there it let out a tremendous screech.

Plumes of smoke spiralled up into the air. The sun peeped over the horizon, lighting up the sky with a blaze of orange as if the whole sky was alight. Two silhouetted pirates fought furiously on deck. The clash of their cutlasses made Otto feel sicker than ever. He recognised the flowing locks of Jethro Silver who towered over the other pirate. Jethro ducked and dived. His feet moved so fast as if he was doing an intricate dance and Otto was sure Jethro would have the other pirate over the side of the galleon at any moment.

"Watch out, Jethro!" cried Florence, joining the monkey on deck. "Behind you!"

Too late, Jethro spun round to find the second pirate, his long beard streaming in the wind, aiming a musket straight at him. The monkey raced across the deck and launched itself at the pirate, landing on the pirate's back. With a roar of rage, the pirate wrenched the monkey off his shoulder and flung it across the deck. The monkey landed in a jangled heap.

"No!" gasped Otto.

Florence threw herself across the deck and scooped up the lifeless monkey. She cradled it in her arms.

Otto's heart beat so fast he was almost breathless. The smaller pirate, who still stood forgotten behind Jethro's back, raised his cutlass in the air and was about to swing it at Jethro's neck.

"No!" screamed Otto. He ran full pelt across the deck, colliding into the pirate with the beard as he aimed the musket. The impact pushed the pirate to the deck, knocking the musket out of his hand and onto Jethro, which threw him off balance. The sweep of the other pirate's cutlass missed Jethro's neck but caught him on his arm. Dark blood seeped through the steam pirate's coat but he didn't wince. He whipped round and caught hold of the skinny pirate and threw him overboard. Otto watched the pirate's stripey legs disappear over the rails and heard an almighty splash.

Otto grabbed the musket which lay on the deck beside him. Clutching it in his trembling hands, he held it out in front of him at the last pirate, his beard now a tangled mess. The wooden pirate ship was well ablaze and its central mast was about to collapse like a fallen tree. Those pirates that had remained on its deck abandoned the burning ship and dived overboard to join the others in the churning sea.

"Looks like we'll make a pirate of you yet," said Jethro Silver, kneeling and looking up. The dark wet patch of blood on his sleeve grew bigger. By the light of the new dawn, Otto saw pain in his father's eyes.

Florence carried the monkey over to where Otto crouched next to his father. The monkey blinked and moved its arms but Otto knew by the awkward position of the monkey's leg that it had been damaged.

"They won't be back," said Jethro. "Not today, anyway."

Chapter 27 – The Longest Night

Otto rested the monkey on the top of a wooden barrel. "The metal inside his leg has snapped," he said.

"Can we fix it?" asked Florence.

"Sure, if we had any wire I could easily bind it together but we don't have any."

"There must be something we could use," said Florence, searching around them on the deck.

"What are you scrabbling around for?" called Jethro.

The sun was high in the sky but Jethro Silver still looked grey. He'd bandaged his arm with a length of cloth but already it was soaked through with blood.

"Wire," called back Otto.

"Try the drawers in my desk," called Jethro. "And get us a hot drink whilst you're at it, there's a nip in the air."

Beads of sweat glistened on the steam pirate's brow.

"You sure he's all right?" whispered Otto. "That wound looks pretty bad."

Florence shrugged. "Let's take a look down below."

Otto cradled the monkey carefully in his arms as he followed Florence. When they reached Jethro Silver's cabin, Florence headed over to the wooden desk that sat at the foot of the bunk. A map stretched across it, weighted down by a pewter tankard and penknife. The cabin reeked of rum and sweat. The lantern that swayed from a hook above the desk shed little light as Florence pulled open one of the drawers and rummaged inside in the gloom.

"I can't see a thing in here," she said. "Hold that lantern closer."

Otto set the monkey down on top of the map and lifted down the lantern. The top drawer was stuffed full of maps, a compass, a bunch of keys and a tarnished fob watch on a long chain.

"Try the other one," said Otto.

The second drawer was very deep and crammed full of old cogs, screws and springs. Florence took out a handful and heaped them on the desk next to the monkey who sat watching.

"Looks just like your uncle's stuff," said Florence, pulling out a screwdriver and a pair of rusty tweezers.

The monkey reached into the drawer and lifted up a square of shiny paper that was sticking out.

"What you got there?" asked Florence, taking the small photograph from the monkey's hand.

"That's a picture of my mother," said Otto. Her face stared back at him. It was creased from having been folded but it showed the same familiar face as in the photograph back in his uncle's study.

"These must be her things," said Otto. He picked up a large spring and uncoiled it until it was a curving length of wire.

The monkey chattered loudly. Florence reached to the back of the drawer and pulled out a small leather notebook tied closed with a length of leather thong.

"Do you think this belonged to your mother too?" asked Florence, untying the bow and opening out the pages which were crinkled and yellowed with age.

"Maybe," said Otto.

The pages were full of writing, beautiful slanted letters, dotted between strange numbers and symbols that Otto didn't recognise. He took the book from Florence. All of a sudden it was too much to bear. His mother, whom Otto could barely remember, must have held those things. After all these years, Jethro had kept them.

Another picture fell out from between the pages. It was the picture of a small boy with a ruffled head of curls and a smudge of dirt on his sun-kissed cheek. Otto realised he was looking at himself, how he once must have looked long before his uncle and the orangery, when he was the son of a pirate. He slipped the picture between the pages and closed the book shut, then he put it back in the drawer along with everything else.

"You okay?" asked Florence.

"Yeah," said Otto, though his eyes brimmed with tears.

"Wish I had a father," said Florence. "I never knew mine."

Otto didn't know his father either. To him, the steam pirate up on deck was still a faded memory, one with more questions than answers. The monkey nudged him and held out the length of wire.

"I'll mend the monkey," said Otto, composing himself. "You boil the water for the tea."

As Florence left the cabin, the monkey touched Otto gently on the arm. Otto was sure he saw something more than light glinting on the creature's glass eyes. He saw a sparkle of life that seemed to understand his pain and Otto realised how very special the monkey really was.

The further north the galleon sailed the colder and stronger the wind blew, pushing them ever nearer Gostopolus Island. The sun slipped beyond the horizon taking with it the last glimmer of warmth. The moon lay shrouded behind deep purple clouds. Jethro Silver could barely stand and what had begun as a tremor in his hands had become a shiver throughout his whole body.

"Time to turn in," he said, supporting himself against the ship's wheel. He tapped a series of buttons. "The course is set, the wind will do the rest." The bandage on his arm was sodden with blood and his face was drained of colour.

Below deck Otto couldn't sleep. Instead of the usual snoring coming from Jethro's cabin, Otto heard the steam pirate muttering in his sleep.

"He's got a fever," said Florence. She sat up in her bunk, her notebook open on her lap. Sweeping lines of charcoal captured the pose of the sleeping monkey who lay curled up by Otto's feet.

Otto remembered the time a couple of years ago when he had lain in bed with a fever. His uncle had sat beside him all night, keeping watch. "What if he's not well enough the steer the galleon. We could be blown anywhere...what if the pirates come back?"

Florence set down her notebook and crawled off her bunk. "Let's go and check on him."

Inside Jethro's cabin, the steam pirate thrashed around, eyes closed. His hair was a wet mass around his face.

"He's burning up," said Florence.

The two of them crouched down beside the steam pirate. Some blood oozed out beneath the bandage on his arm, staining the bed sheet beneath.

"You stay here," said Florence. "I'll get a basin of water."

Jethro turned over and threw out his arm, thumping Otto on the shoulder.

"Otto, is that you?"

Jethro's lips were dry and cracked and his eyes had a glazed look about them.

"Your arm's still bleeding," said Otto.

"It'll mend," muttered Jethro. "You should have seen the blood when I lost my eye. My arm's just a scratch."

Otto looked at the sweat which glistened along the jagged scar across Jethro's cheek and the puckered skin where once his left eye had been.

Jethro clutched Otto's hand.

"Emoria Cogwright's a demon with a cutlass. She took this eye out with a single swipe of her blade."

Otto caught his breath.

Jethro turned away and closed his eye.

"You said it was a shark," said Otto.

"I say a lot of things," mumbled Jethro. He turned his head. "Can't go letting people know I let someone like Emoria do this. I have a reputation." Jethro tried to laugh but it turned to a cough, so rough that Otto feared he may never stop.

At last Jethro opened his eye wide and pulled Otto closer.

"Between you and me, it wasn't a fair fight. I didn't see the blade coming. I was..." Jethro stopped talking and swallowed hard.

"What happened?" prompted Otto.

"Your mother was injured, it all happened so fast. One minute she was holding her parrot, the next she was swept up so high... She fell... Really badly. I just wanted to help her. I wanted her to move but she just kept calling your name... Over and over... Until she could say no more."

Jethro fell silent, his breathing laboured. A shiver ran straight through him. A clatter in the doorway made Otto turn around.

Florence had pushed open the door with her foot. Carefully she carried a metal basin of water across the cabin to the bunk. Water sloshed over the side of the basin as the galleon was rocked by the sea.

Florence dipped a piece of cloth into the water and mopped the steam pirate's forehead. Then she removed the bandage from Jethro's arm and carefully cleaned the wound. Each time she returned the cloth to the basin, blood swirled in the water turning it red.

Otto couldn't take in what Jethro had said. Emoria Cogwright. She'd stolen the parrots and kidnapped her uncle and now... Had she killed his mother too? Otto wanted to tell Florence but he just couldn't put it into words. His mind was fizzing with questions.

Florence tied a new strip of cloth around Jethro's arm.

"Will he... Will he be all right?" stammered Otto.

"We'll know by morning," Florence replied. "I'll get clean water."

Jethro's breathing had eased and again he reached for Otto's hand and squeezed it. "I'm so very sorry," he said. "Your uncle blamed me when your mother died and he never forgave me. When I thought I could lose nothing more, he took you... Stole you away and I thought I'd never find you again."

Chapter 28 – The Greeting Party

After a couple of days Jethro Silver's fever broke and his arm began to heal. Otto stayed close to his father. Florence, who had sensed she was in the way, spent her days fishing over the side of the galleon, scrubbing the decks and re-organising the galley kitchen below. Though Otto and Jethro chatted often, the steam pirate never again mentioned the day Otto's mother had died and Otto didn't want to push him.

Day after day they sailed nearer to Gostopolus Island, where Emoria Cogwright had taken his uncle. Otto couldn't stop thinking about all the lies his uncle had told. Delderfield Macauley hadn't been protecting him from a dangerous world outside, he'd been hiding him as a prisoner so his father would never find him. All this time Otto had been the son of a pirate and a brilliant inventor and he'd never known.

"Why don't you go help Florence mend the fishing net?" Jethro stood at the wheel, his cheeks once again flushed with colour.

"But I could help you. You said yourself I've the making of a true sailor. You could teach me to steer."

"You don't need to watch over me, Otto. You're an excellent nurse maid, just like your mother but I'm good, really. Florence could do with your company. She's run out of things to draw and this galleon has never been so clean."

Florence sat cross-legged on the deck darning a massive hole in a tatty fishing net with a bone needle and a length of twine. She'd tied her long, shaggy hair behind her neck with a strip of cotton fabric and was concentrating so hard she hadn't noticed her glasses had slipped down her nose. The sun had grown fiercer with every day and the deck was uncomfortably hot under Otto's bare feet.

Otto leaned over the side of the galleon, still reluctant to leave Jethro's side. A heat haze shimmered over the emerald ocean. The monkey ran towards him across the deck and up onto his shoulder.

"You did a great repair on that monkey's leg," called Jethro. "Your mother would have been proud."

He could fashion a repair and paint his uncle's mechanical birds but Otto knew he was nothing like his mother. Surely she was the one who had created the heart which beat inside the monkey's chest, the heart that brought it alive just like the parrots. It was a secret that Emoria Cogwright would do anything to acquire.

"It was the parrot that Emoria Cogwright wanted, wasn't it?" asked Otto, squeezing the monkey tightly.

"She always wants what she can't have," said Jethro, steering the galleon into the wind.

"Did she take it? Mum's parrot?"

"She took your mother away from me and she may as well have taken you but the parrot lies somewhere near here, on the seabed where it fell. Now get going, we'll be at Gostopolus Island within the hour."

"Can we see it?" Otto peered at the horizon, shading his eyes from the glare of the sun and there was the island, a smudge of brown hiding behind the haze.

"Don't go thinking it'll be easy Otto. I'll need my crew, all three of you."

The monkey chattered.

Otto relayed the story Jethro had told him. Florence listened intently as she sewed.

"Emoria Cogwright cut out his eye!" exclaimed Florence. She tied off the twine and inspected the finished fishing net.

"Maybe we shouldn't have come," said Otto. "How are we ever going to take on Emoria Cogwright?"

"Hey, that's not fighting talk," cried Florence, piling the fishing net neatly beside her. "You've got pirate blood, Jethro Silver is a notorious steam pirate and I don't like bullies."

"She's dangerous," said Otto.

The monkey barred its teeth.

"She's just one against three, even if she does have a few clever tricks up her sleeves. You'll see."

But Otto felt a deep uneasiness in the pit of his stomach. There was something Jethro wasn't telling him, something that didn't make sense. What had he said? His mother had fallen a great height, how was that even possible and what had it to do with Emoria Cogwright?

"Land ahoy!" called Jethro Silver. "Get ready, crew. Gather your weapons and brace yourselves for landing."

Jethro tucked his musket in his shoulder holster under his jacket and pushed his cutlass down the side of his boot.

"What about us?" said Florence.

Jethro handed each of them a sturdy stick, almost as tall as they were and slipped a penknife into Otto's pocket. "Don't use it unless you have to," he whispered in Otto's ear.

The monkey curled itself around Otto's neck and chattered loudly.

"It's going to be a wet landing," said Jethro.

Gostopolus Island loomed up at them, a vast expanse of volcanic rock where few trees grew. Those that did had been twisted and beaten sideways by the strong wind which whipped waves around them into white seahorses that galloped onto the pebbly shore.

"Doesn't look like there's much there," said Florence.

"Don't be fooled and keep your eyes peeled. Nothing is as it seems here. There's a reason no one who's been here ever leaves to tell the tale."

Jethro sailed the galleon into a small secluded bay and there he dropped anchor. He lowered the gangplank into the churning water. He scooped up the monkey and held it high above his head, leading the way down the gangplank. Water swirled around his legs. Otto and Florence kept close behind him, steadying themselves with their sticks. Their legs were soon soaked up to their knees as water sprayed over them. Ashore the pebbles glistened and Otto's boots squelched as he followed Jethro Silver up the beach.

At first Otto thought they were alone, surrounded only by rocks weathered into ugly formations.

"Keep close," warned Jethro Silver, passing the monkey back to Otto.

Otto shivered. Though the sun shone, a brisk wind whipped over the beach and beat his wet trousers against his legs. There was something eerie about Gostopolus Island. He was sure they were being watched. Then he saw them: eyes peeped out of every crevice. They peered from behind the weathered trees and lurked in caves carved into the rocks.

A large mechanical crab scuttled out from between two rocks. It crawled across the stones and snapped its copper pincers. It was followed by a whole tide of mechanical crabs that crept sideways towards Otto, their glass eyes on stalks following every step Otto took.

A clatter of falling stones made Otto spin round.

"Watch out!" cried Jethro. "Run!"

From behind a wall of rock, a gigantic octopus rose above them. Its articulated tentacles pulled it along the beach. Rows of pulsating metal suckers gripped the rocks in its path. A huge bulbous head was fashioned from metal sheets crudely bolted together and two humongous green eyes glinted in the sunlight.

Chapter 29 – The Mechanical Zoo

Otto ran. The wet pebbles shifted beneath his feet.

"What is that?" cried Florence, sprinting close behind.

The monkey gripped tightly onto Otto's neck and screeched loudly.

"Emoria's secret weapon," called Jethro. He'd reached the top of the beach and now began hauling himself up the rocks. "Climb higher," he called. "It won't be able to keep up."

Otto scrambled up the large boulders, using his stick to heave himself up. He soon realised there was a path of sorts woven between the rocks, which were wet to the touch from the ocean spray and smelt of seaweed and rotting fish. The octopus followed. Sucker by sucker it hauled itself up the rocks. Its hulk threw a dark shadow across Otto's path. The clink of metal against stone made Otto's heart beat even faster.

Soon they could climb no higher. Above them stretched a sheer rock face which rose up to a clear turquoise sky.

Otto heard the beating of wings above him and looked up to see a large gull. Its breast was a blaze of silver and its wings, layer upon layer of hammered metal feathers set onto articulated metal struts. The gull's wings beat the air majestically, lifting the bird high above them. Its razor sharp bill could surely skewer any living thing.

Otto stumbled and his foot slipped. He landed badly, grazing his knee. Florence took Otto's arm to steady him.

Jethro looked back. "There's no way up. We'll have to climb across these rocks and head back down the beach."

What kind of place is this, thought Otto. It looked like some hideous mechanical zoo. Each creature, though meticulously engineered, was somehow ugly. Not like his uncle's beautiful painted birds. These creatures belonged in bad nightmares, the kind that left you still shaken the morning after.

Far below them stretched the beach and the steam galleon rocked in the bay. To Otto's horror the octopus had changed course. It stretched its tentacles over the rocks and heaved itself closer. From where Otto stood, the crabs below looked like a swarm of ants on the beach. The gull, still flying above Otto, was joined by another and they began to circle, as if eyeing up their prey. There was nothing for it but to follow Jethro.

The monkey squeezed tighter around Otto's neck.

"It'll be alright," whispered Otto, though he didn't believe it himself. His uncle was somewhere on this island, though it was hard to see where. There had been no sign of Emoria's Golden Serpent when they landed, so where had she moored her ship? There were just rocks for as far as Otto could see.

"Maybe your uncle's not here at all. Maybe Emoria isn't either," said Florence. He kept close to Otto now. "Unless he's in one of those caves. You were right, maybe we shouldn't have come here."

Jethro Silver stopped up ahead, waiting until they caught up. "Oh, she's here alright," he said. "I can feel her."

"What did you mean when you said that octopus was Emoria's secret weapon?" asked Otto, glad of the rest. His knee throbbed and his feet ached. The sun blazed down from a cloudless sky and he'd never felt so thirsty.

For a moment, Jethro Silver looked like he wasn't going to answer. He looked down. They'd rounded a corner of the island and the beach below them was now an expanse of golden sand. Beads of sweat glistened above Jethro's eyebrows and he wiped his forehead with his sleeve.

"That octopus killed your mother. There was nothing I could do. She screamed your name over and over again as it dangled her out of my reach. Then it dropped her..."

114

Otto's blood ran cold. Suddenly he felt so very weak he had to sit down. He slumped on the rocks. The monkey squatted down and patted Otto on the cheek and squeezed his hand.

Florence turned to look behind them. "Hey, that octopus has stopped following us."

"Oh it will be waiting," said Jethro. "It follows the sound. It can't see us."

Otto cradled the monkey in his lap.

"Those hunks of metal are nothing but mechanical toys. They can't think or feel, not like your monkey or your uncle's parrots. I don't know how your mother did it but somehow she breathed life into her creatures."

"What do we do now?" asked Otto, pulling himself to his feet.

The monkey ran along ahead, its tail held high.

"Follow the monkey," laughed Jethro. "It's as good a way as any. Maybe we've been looking in the wrong place. Like Florence said, let's look in those caves down there."

Jethro pointed to the sandy beach and the row of caves set on the rocky shore. Behind them the sound of metal clanked against stone. The octopus was following. The cliff was not so steep lower down and Florence raced ahead overtaking the monkey. She leapt the last couple of feet to the beach beneath. Otto joined her and his feet sunk into soft sand that filled his boots.

"Get a move on," called Jethro, striding past them across the sand.

Above them, the gulls continued to circle like seabirds around a fishing boat. Otto was sure something else was following them but when he whipped around there was nothing there, just boulders dotted along the shore. They'd nearly reached the first cave when the monkey froze. It leaned its head on one side and listened. Otto heard it too, the sound of something being dragged. It echoed inside the entrance of the first cave.

The monkey screeched.

Seconds later a mechanical walrus manoeuvred itself out of the shadows of the cave and pulled itself up to its full height. It clapped its flippers. Its tusks were tubes of thick shiny metal and its body a mass of rusted metal plates. Out from behind the walrus scurried a gang of little seabirds, propelled at terrific speed by their tiny mechanical legs.

Above Otto's head the gulls beat their wings. Otto caught his breath.

"Looks like we have ourselves a greeting party," said Jethro.

Noises behind him made Otto spin around. An army of giant crabs had formed a semi-circle around them. In the distance, Otto spotted the octopus which had reached the bottom of the cliff. It stretched its tentacles out across the sand.

"I've been expecting you," came a voice from inside the entrance to the cave. "Your uncle will be pleased."

The shadow of the figure emerged first but Otto recognised the voice. Emoria Cogwright. Her goggles whirred as she strode out into the sunlight, her red curls more vibrant than ever. Her golden lizard crawled out of her pocket and slithered down her leg to the sand where it flicked out its tongue. The monkey swatted it with its hand.

"Welcome to my mechanical zoo," said Emoria. She knelt down in front of the monkey and reached out her hand to stroke it but the monkey reared up on its hind legs and screeched.

The shadow of a gull flew over Otto's head and before he had time to yell out a warning, the gull snatched up the monkey. With a beat of its wings, the gull flew into the mouth of the cave, carrying the terrified monkey with it.

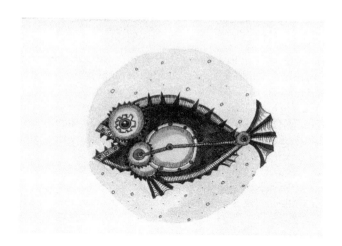

Chapter 30 – The Essence of Life

"Jethro, how touching. You've come to rescue the parrots that remind you of Natisha. Or have you come to find your childhood friend?"

"Where's my uncle?" cut in Otto.

"Oh the pirate boy, how brave and foolish you've become, just like your father."

"That's enough Emoria. We'll be taking Delderfield and his parrots and we'll be leaving." Jethro ushered Otto and Florence behind him.

"Talking of Delderfield, he's become quite uncooperative. Maybe you can talk some sense into him."

"Where is he?" said Florence. She pushed beside Jethro.

Emoria's goggles whirred and zoomed out further, eyeing up the girl.

"Been training your new crew, I see, Jethro. I'll take you to him."

Jethro pulled the cutlass from his boot and flashed it in front of Emoria's face. "No tricks this time."

Emoria raised her arms in the air and clicked her fingers. The crabs scuttled closer until their pincers were snapping at Otto's legs. The octopus was close behind blocking the exit back to the beach.

"Follow me," said Emoria.

She led them into the cave. Out of the sun it suddenly felt very cold. Otto shivered. He turned back to see the walrus standing guard at the entrance to the cave. The gaggle of seabirds ran back past Otto into the cave, nearly tripping him over. Their clockwork legs carried them away into the darkness.

Emoria stopped outside a set of enormous metal doors and pushed a button protruding from a rock beside them. Seconds later the doors pinged open to reveal a large metal room.

"Hurry up inside," she called. "Before the doors close."

Jethro pulled the children inside just in time and the doors snapped shut behind them. The metal room shot downwards and Otto's stomach plummeted to his feet.

"It's an elevator," laughed Emoria. "You didn't really think I lived in a cave, did you? It's a clever invention operated by an elaborate system of pulleys. It's so much cosier down here, just you wait and see."

Much to Otto's relief the elevator came to an abrupt stop and the doors opened again. Emoria marched into a brightly lit corridor. A festoon of lanterns hung suspended from the ceiling. She picked her way through what at first sight appeared to be a collection of large stones that were scattered along the floor. As Otto stepped over them he noticed they moved, really slowly. They weren't stones at all. From rusted metal shells sprung stubby legs and grotesque heads. Their gaping mouths gulped the air around them.

"Mind the turtles," called Emoria.

A large glass tank of water took up most of one wall. Inside swam a huge mechanical crocodile. Its glass eyes blinked above the water line and its legs propelled it along the tank. The crocodile was surrounded by the weirdest and ugliest fish Otto had ever seen. Their eyes were large cogs and jagged metal formed rows of menacing teeth. Articulated fins allowed them to swim through the algae-coloured water.

Emoria stopped and tapped the side of the tank. The crocodile turned towards her and peered over the side of the tank. Emoria reached over and patted the crocodile's head.

"Just some visitors my lovelies, nothing to worry about."

The crocodile stared back blankly.

"Where's Delderfield?" asked Jethro.

"And my monkey?" shouted Otto.

"Patience. Have you nothing to say? You are privileged to see my wonderful collection, my life's work. Every creature you see here is a beautiful discovery. They come from the four corners of the known world. The crocodile here is from the furthest region of the tropics. Isn't he magnificent?"

Emoria's goggles zoomed out towards Otto and she leaned closer. "I saved him from a grotty basement. Here he will soon have the run of the island. A bit of fine tuning and he'll be ready for release, won't you darling." Emoria tickled the crocodile under the chin and it thrashed its tail.

"You mean you stole it, Emoria, just like you stole Delderfield's parrots," said Jethro.

"I like to think of it as... Re-homing. These creatures deserve better. Not all of them arrive in such great shape. Many have languished in scrapheaps or simply been left to rust away. Come, I'll show you."

Emoria led them through a doorway and down a corridor into another much larger chamber. One whole side was taken up by a series of workbenches. Each contained a menagerie of mechanical animals in various stages of repair. It was the most macabre sight Otto had ever seen.

Rusted body parts lay in huge piles. An elephant lay on its back, its mechanical innards spewed over the bench around it like an interrupted operation. The skeletal frame of a giraffe towered above them, its metal coated in rust. Birds minus wings and animals missing heads and limbs lay lifeless side by side amongst a horde of tools, cogs and springs. It was like a giant surgical suite for misfits and oddities. But it was what lay beyond it that made Otto cry out.

In amongst all the dark, dirty metal stood a large cage and inside that his uncle's six mechanical parrots were a brilliant flash of colour in the gloom. The parrots flew agitatedly from one side of the cage to the other, their magnificent orange and blue wings spread wide. Otto couldn't believe he'd finally found them. "Let them go!" he cried.

"They'll soon settle down," said Emoria. She reached her hand through the metal bars of the cage and tried to touch one of the parrots but it nipped her hard with its beak.

"I don't think it likes you," laughed Jethro. He put his arm around Otto's shoulder. "Unlike all these other creatures, the parrots can see you for what you really are."

"Look"!" pointed Florence, gesturing upwards.

119

There, hunched on the top of the cage sat the monkey. When he spotted Otto, the monkey stood up on its hind legs and clapped its hands. The parrots squawked.

"The monkey will make a wonderful addition to my collection, don't you think?" asked Emoria.

The monkey blew a raspberry.

The fear that had swamped Otto when they entered the cave now erupted into anger. "You can't keep it!"

"What a feisty little pirate you have there, Jethro," laughed Emoria. "You must be very proud."

A sound behind Otto made him turn around. The mechanical lizard slithered along the floor towards where Emoria stood.

"Oh there you are, do hurry up," said Emoria. She bent down, scooped up the lizard and kissed the top of its head before popping it back inside her coat pocket.

"I want to see my uncle," demanded Otto.

Emoria stooped to Otto's height and her goggles zoomed out further to get a better look at him.

"I'm afraid Delderfield is very busy."

"What 'ave you done to him?" accused Florence, pushing her way forward so that she stood directly before her. She thrust out her stick and waved it like a sword.

"He's getting ready for a very important operation," said Emoria. "I've waited so very long for this day and you've arrived just in time. In fact Otto, you should help him, it'll be just like old times for you." Emoria stood up. "Delderfield," she called. "Come out here, we have guests."

Otto hadn't noticed a small door to the right of the parrot cage but now he heard the door swing open. In walked his uncle, his hair ruffled and his suit somewhat creased. In his arms he carried the black metal box. Emoria threw open its lid. Inside beat the purple blob.

Florence's eyes opened wide. Jethro caught his breath. Otto could only stare at the beating mass, the very same that he had found in his uncle's study and that Emoria had stolen. It formed the heart which beat within the monkey who screeched from the top of the cage.

"What are you going to do?" asked Otto.

"Breathe life into my greatest friend of course," said Emoria. "So that he may love me, the way that I love him."

120

The lizard popped its head out of Emoria's pocket and flicked out its tongue. She patted the lizard's head. "Oh no, not him."

Behind Otto came the sound of metal suckers on the stone floor. The blood drained from Jethro's face.

Otto spun round. He felt the hairs on his arms tingle and suddenly his legs felt too weak to hold him.

"It seems Natisha developed a substance so powerful it can form not only a beating heart, but it gives its recipient the very essence of life; a soul which allows the recipient to think for itself and to love."

The octopus stretched out its tentacles and dragged itself nearer.

Only the monkey saw the look of horror on Delderfield Macauley's face.

Chapter 31 – The Octopus

The monkey screeched and bared its porcelain teeth. The parrots squawked in unison and the octopus pulled itself closer. Otto felt so sick he thought he might actually faint. His uncle began to sway, his face ashen white. His hands shook and he struggled to hold the metal box.

Emoria chuckled. "You should be proud of your sister, Delderfield. What she invented is not just pure genius, it revolutionises mechanics. It makes creatures so like the real thing that only their metal construction makes them still a machine. Don't tell me you don't approve?"

Otto's uncle didn't reply.

Emoria leaned closer. "I think you're jealous."

Delderfield couldn't take his eyes off the octopus.

"Jealous your sister had such a gift. You clearly admire it, just look at the parrots you re-created, not to mention the monkey."

Emoria's goggles zoomed so close to Delderfield's face that they nearly touched the end of his nose.

"You may have an eye for colour but it was Natisha who could breathe life into metal. You took her greatest invention for yourself the day you stole her son."

Delderfield dropped the metal box with a clatter onto the floor. Inside the purple blob shuddered.

"I didn't steal him," cried Delderfield.

Otto caught his breath. Out of the corner of his eye he saw the monkey creep down the side of the parrot cage. There the monkey stopped and held one finger to its lips.

"I rescued Otto from a man who had no idea how to keep my sister safe." Delderfield's voice quivered. He steadied himself against a workbench. "He's a steam pirate, wanted for crimes across the oceans. Just look at what he let happen to her... My beautiful sister."

Otto had never seen his uncle cry but now a fat tear cascaded down Delderfield's cheek.

"He was your best friend," said Emoria.

Florence nudged Otto. The monkey was slipping a piece of wire into the lock of the cage.

"Some friend he turned out to be," said Delderfield.

The octopus loomed above them, now so near that it cast a shadow across the children. The creature's huge glass eyes were a shade of green so cold that they made Otto shiver.

Jethro clapped loudly. "Bravo Emoria. You tell tales better than any pirate. What other lies have you fed poor Delderfield?"

There had been so many lies already, Otto was beginning to feel sorry for his uncle. Otto spun from Jethro to Emoria, positioning himself in front of the cage door so no-one could see the monkey picking the lock. One of the octopus's tentacles wrapped itself around Otto's leg. He froze. What felt like a heavy stone weighted his stomach and he began to sweat. He daren't move. The hulk of the octopus stood beside him and there was nowhere to go.

"We couldn't have the world realising that Jethro Silver, the notorious steam pirate, had allowed a woman to melt his heart, now could we?" said Emoria. "I bet you haven't told anyone how you really lost that eye, have you Jethro?"

Jethro narrowed his eye and clenched the cutlass in his hand.

The tentacle tightened around Otto's ankle, pinching his skin. Florence gestured with her head towards the parrot cage as the door clicked open. Otto kicked Jethro with his other foot. The parrots squawked. Jethro looked to where Florence gestured her head.

"If anyone is to blame for Natisha's death, it's you, Emoria," said Jethro. "You and that giant scrapheap."

The octopus blinked its eyes.

Emoria cleared her throat. "I didn't mean it to..."

"No!" interrupted Jethro. He grabbed Emoria by the arm and pulled her to one side where she couldn't see the door to the parrot cage click open or the monkey's triumphant grin. "It was you who wanted Natisha's invention and your octopus who killed her. You always want what's not yours to have."

Delderfield's eyes widened and his moustache stiffened.

"Go on, tell him, or shall I?"

"You... You killed Natisha? For what... For this?" Delderfield kicked the metal box.

"And when I tried to save Natisha, Emoria sliced out my eye!" bellowed Jethro.

Delderfield's face flushed bright red and for a second Otto thought his uncle might actually explode, but whatever his uncle was about to say was drowned out by the tremendous beating of metal wings. All six mechanical parrots swooped out of the cage and lunged for Emoria.

Chapter 32 – Pandemonium of Parrots

Emoria Cogwright's screams echoed around the chamber. One by one the parrots swooped at her head. They pecked her red curls as her arms wind-milled around her head. She tried to beat the parrots away but soon they covered her, flashes of red, orange and blue. All that was left visible were her feet sticking out below.

"Run!" cried Florence, taking Otto's hand.

"I can't," replied Otto. He pointed to the tentacle wrapped tightly around his ankle.

Jethro grabbed hold of Delderfield. "We're getting out of here, now!" he cried.

Emoria's piercing screech hurt Otto's ears. The octopus blinked. Raising its tentacles high in the air it released its hold on Otto's ankle. The monkey clapped hysterically then raced along the floor ahead of Otto and scooted past the octopus.

"Help!" Emoria thrashed her arms furiously, hitting out at everything she touched.

"This way!" called Jethro, dragging Delderfield behind him.

"But I can't leave without my parrots," he wailed.

"Oh yes you can," snarled Jethro, tugging harder.

The octopus responded to Emoria's shrieks. It hurled its tentacles towards the writhing mass of parrots and plucked one out of the air.

With a squawk, the parrot was propelled across the chamber and sailed past Otto's head. Seconds later the squawking parrot was joined by another.

"Duck!" shouted Florence, just as a parrot catapulted over her head.

"There's no escape!" screeched Emoria.

Florence dodged past the octopus and headed towards the doorway through which earlier Emoria had shown them. The monkey had already scampered through it.

Twhack! Another parrot went flying. It did a loop the loop in mid-air, regained control and swept back across the chamber, striking Emoria squarely on the forehead.

The octopus lashed out another tentacle and swiped the parrot so hard it spun in the air before crashing to the floor.

"No! I have to go back," cried Delderfield. He wrangled his arm free from Jethro's grip and sprinted back to where the parrot lay with a broken wing.

"Leave it!" bellowed Jethro. "Watch out!"

The octopus whipped a tentacle into the air and brought it crashing down, missing Delderfield by a whisper as he ran with the injured parrot stuffed under his arm.

Dazed, Emoria didn't notice the remaining three mechanical parrots flying up behind her. Each grabbed hold of her. One clutched onto her hair, the other two grasped the shoulders of her coat in their talons. With an almighty beating of their wings they hoisted the startled Emoria off the floor.

"Put me down!" she shrieked.

Jethro stuffed his cutlass back in his boot. He seized hold of Delderfield's arm again and pulled him towards Otto, who was edging his way past the octopus, following Florence's lead. Otto had almost caught up with her when the octopus heard his footsteps. It flung a tentacle out in front of him, tripping Otto over like a rope, catching his foot. Down he fell with an almighty crash.

Emoria dangled beneath the parrots' grasp. Wildly, she kicked her legs. Otto pulled himself back up but when he tried to put weight on his left foot he yelped in pain. His ankle throbbed and gave way. Jethro let go of Delderfield and stooped to heave Otto up off the floor.

Otto looked up into his uncle's eyes.

"I didn't realise," muttered Delderfield. "I thought... If I'd known, I..."

126

"No time for apologies, Delderfield," cut in Jethro as he hauled Otto along, one arm firmly around his son's shoulder. "Give us a hand."

Delderfield took Otto's other arm. With their help, Otto hobbled along. Above them Emoria twisted and turned. She lashed out at the octopus beneath her, whacking it on the head with her foot.

The octopus jerked upwards. It shot out one tentacle, then another, smacking one parrot so hard it was forced to release its grip on Emoria's hair.

"Hurry," called Jethro, but they had barely squeezed past the octopus when Emoria roared in triumph. She sailed through the air, free of her coat, leaving the remaining parrots clutching nothing but leather. She landed on one of the octopus's tentacles and slid down it so fast she flew off the other end and landed with a bump on her bottom. She skidded along the floor and knocked Jethro over like a nine pin.

Otto flew out of Delderfield's hold and landed face down. He was joined seconds later by his uncle. Unable to drag himself up in time, Otto could only look in horror as Emoria lunged at Delderfield. The parrot, still lodged under his arm, squawked and wriggled free.

"You have work to do, Delderfield," spat Emoria, kneeling on his chest, pinning him to the floor.

"Get off of him!" cried Otto. He tugged at Emoria's shoulders but she shoved him away.

Jethro pulled himself up. Too late, he reached for the cutlass tucked in his boot but Emoria had already snatched it. She jabbed it towards his face.

"You're getting slow, Jethro."

Florence looked helplessly back at them.

"Up you get Delderfield." Emoria pulled Otto's uncle to his feet.

Otto saw Jethro reach for the musket strapped around his chest.

"Oh no you don't, not if you want your son alive," cried Emoria. She yanked Otto by her side and backed away slowly.

Delderfield took hold of Otto's hand. Never before in all the years they had been together had Otto valued his uncle's touch. Now he squeezed his hand in return.

"We'll see about that," said Jethro, a smile creasing across his face. "It's not that easy to get rid of me." He rushed towards them.

Emoria grabbed a metal cog up off the floor and slung it like a boomerang. It missed Jethro's head by a hair's width and clattered to the floor.

"That all you've got?" jeered Jethro, raising his musket.

But the octopus heard the cog fall and swung out a tentacle that whipped Jethro off his feet, sending the musket flying through the air. Only the monkey saw Florence hiding beyond the doorway but the octopus heard her cry and lumbered forwards towards the sound, reaching out its tentacles.

Jethro crawled to his feet but the octopus blocked his way. As the rusted hulk dragged itself towards the sound of Florence's voice, Jethro was squeezed back against the wall until he was wedged fast.

The monkey heard Jethro's cries and raced back into the chamber. Florence followed. Together they clambered over the octopus, dodging the reach of its tentacles and stopped short of where Emoria stood with Delderfield, arguing.

"I won't help you," cried Delderfield.

"Jethro!" screamed Otto. Standing beside his uncle he could no longer see the steam pirate behind the octopus but he could hear his cursing. What if he was crushed? What if he couldn't breathe? He couldn't lose his father, not now, not when he'd only just found him.

Emoria spun round. She tightened her grip on Otto's arm. With a screech the monkey launched itself at Emoria.

"Get off me!" she cried.

Otto wriggled free and started to crawl towards Jethro who was still trapped. In that second the monkey hung onto Emoria's neck and whisked off her goggles. Otto heard her scream and turned to look. What he saw made the blood drain from his face. Delderfield gasped. The goggles clattered to the floor. The monkey shrieked triumphantly.

The octopus pulled away from the wall and Jethro slumped to the floor.

Otto stared at Emoria. Where her goggles had been sat two tiny shrunken white eyes sunk into deep dark hollows. They blindly stared in Otto's direction.

Emoria grappled on the floor until her hands found her goggles.

"You can't..." gasped Otto.

Emoria lifted her goggles back over her head and snapped them back into place. They whirred into position and zoomed out to where Otto stood open mouthed.

"But you're..."

Emoria hoisted up one trouser leg and shook her foot towards him. Beneath the fabric was an intricately engineered leg of complex struts and springs.

"I prefer to think of myself as mechanically repaired and refurbished," said Emoria.

Chapter 33 – The Swarm

"You're one of them," cried Otto.

"A machine," said Florence.

The monkey chattered.

"Oh I'm a lot more than a machine," laughed Emoria. "I have the best of both worlds."

Jethro dusted himself down and squeezed past the octopus.

"What are you then?" asked Delderfield. He held the broken parrot in the crook of his arm and gently he stroked its head.

"I'm whatever I want to be," spat Emoria.

"I always thought there was something odd about you," said Jethro, making his way over to Otto's side.

Otto, relieved his father hadn't been squashed to death, squeezed Jethro's hand.

"I may have been abandoned in an orphanage like an unwanted broken doll but at least the Governor was an inventor. He repaired me, as he so crudely put it, but at the time I wished he hadn't."

"That's no quick fix," said Delderfield, peering over the top of his glasses. "That's precision engineering."

"Only the best Delderfield. Of course, little of the original work remains."

Otto heard the distant flap of wings behind them and out of the corner of his eye he saw a flash of red and blue. Oblivious, Emoria scooped the lizard out of her pocket.

"Children are cruel, nasty beasts." She glared at Otto and Florence. "Just as my parents rejected me, so the other kids shunned me, made fun of me. But I didn't need them. I don't need anyone." She kissed the golden lizard on the head.

Otto felt the monkey brush past his leg and saw it dart across the chamber. Behind them Otto heard the octopus inching closer.

"Machines are much more reliable, don't you think? So less cruel. Who needs a human family when I have my own, right here and thanks to Natisha, they will soon love me as much as I love them. I will..."

An almighty crash shook the chamber. Emoria spun round. The mechanical parrots swooped in a frenzy over a pile of junk, like seagulls over a rubbish dump. They plucked up lumps of metal in their talons and let them drop. Cogs and dismembered limbs pounded the workbench and the floor. Jethro grabbed hold of Otto's arm and pushed him forwards. The octopus threw out its tentacles and dragged itself towards the clattering and clashing of metal. The monkey hurled a decapitated owl's head onto the floor then clapped its hands with glee. Otto couldn't help but smile.

The octopus dragged itself closer still.

"Run!" cried Jethro. "Clever one, that monkey of yours."

Delderfield tucked the broken parrot firmly under his arm, took Otto's hand and together they ran and hobbled, their path to the door now free.

Crash! Smash! Bang! Clatter!

The parrots squawked and the monkey screeched triumphantly.

"No!" howled Emoria. "It's a trick!"

But the octopus ignored her cries and dragged itself over to the other side of the chamber as the noise of the parrots grew to a crescendo.

Jethro led the way. Otto, Florence and Delderfeld hurried along behind. Together they raced through the doorway, out of the chamber and past the crocodile tank. They headed towards the metal elevator, the doors of which stood open.

Emoria flew after them. Just as they reached the elevator, Emoria lunged for a control panel set into the wall that Otto hadn't noticed

131

before. She pounded her fist against it. The doors of the elevator slid shut.

In a panic, Otto repeatedly tapped the button next to the elevator doors but they refused to open. Otto heard Emoria chuckling behind them. He desperately looked for another way out and that's when he noticed a metal door further along the wall. Oddly it had no handle at all but when he pushed hard against it he nearly toppled over when it suddenly swung open.

"This way," he called, regaining his balance.

Jethro, Florence and Delderfield darted through it. Otto followed. When he looked back, Emoria stood still, watching them. She made no attempt to follow them. In fact, she looked unnervingly pleased about something as she stroked the lizard that sat on the palm of her hand.

The door led Otto and the others down a stone tunnel. Gas lamps cast shadows that danced across the walls which stank of sea water like a rock pool at low tide.

"What if this doesn't lead anywhere?" said Delderfield. He was so close behind that Otto could feel his uncle's breath on his own cheek, could feel the parrot's feathers poking him in his side.

"Of course it leads somewhere," said Jethro, surging ahead. "Step it up a bit or you'll have Emoria on your tail."

Otto heard a really odd sound. At first he thought it was coming from the walls but then he realised everything echoed in the tunnel so the sound could be coming from anywhere. He spotted a glint of metal on the ground by Florence's feet.

"Stop!" he cried, tugging at Florence who was about to step on it.

"Whoah!" cried Florence.

Delderfield let out a low wail and began hopping from one foot to another.

"It's just a ..." began Jethro.

"A scorpion!" howled Florence.

Otto's heart pounded. He pinned himself back against the wall. In front of them scurried three mechanical scorpions, each with an articulated sting curled up above its head. Their army of little legs scuttled along the rock floor.

Jethro raised his foot to stamp on one.

"What if it's got a real sting?" exclaimed Florence.

"Ahh, good point. Quiet then," hushed Jethro, "Everyone keep back against the wall," he whispered. He tip-toed past the scorpions. "They can't see you, they have no eyes."

Otto's skin crawled. Even when they'd edged safely past them he still flinched with every step he took, his eyes peeled to the ground for more. He was still intently looking at his feet when a new sort of sound echoed through the tunnel.

"Duck!" yelled Jethro.

A loud buzzing was heading towards them.

The sight of a swarm of swooping, darting things flying toward them made Otto's legs tremble beneath him. His palms broke out in a sweat. Jethro bundled him against his chest, wrapping his arms tightly around Otto who struggled to catch his breath.

"Get off of me!" hollered Delderfield, batting his hands above his head.

Florence snatched off her boot, and hopping around on one leg she swatted at the gleaming mass of mechanical insects. Otto peered out between Jethro's hands.

Wasps!

Twenty, thirty, maybe more. They had bulbous striped thorax and evil glass eyes. Their tiny metal wings angrily beat the air.

"Got one!" cried Florence, smacking a wasp against the stone wall of the tunnel where it shattered into tiny pieces.

Thwack! Thwack! Thwack!

Again and again Florence lashed out. She smashed the wasps until they fell into a shower of fragments.

"Emoria knew," breathed Otto. "That's why she didn't follow."

"Well she clearly underestimated Florence," laughed Jethro, tapping Florence on the back.

Florence jumped up and down on the pile of broken metal but her laughter soon fell silent.

A roar, unlike anything Otto had ever heard, engulfed the tunnel. It shook the very ground they stood on.

Jethro froze.

Delderfield fell to his knees, clutching the now squawking parrot.

Otto stared in terror at the shadow which stretched longer and taller along the tunnel wall. When he glimpsed the source of the shadow he thought his heart may stop beating altogether in fright. Facing him, just feet away, was a mechanical lion. Its mane was an explosion of metal fronds, its legs so powerful it could surely leap over anything that moved. Jagged metal teeth glinted in the lamplight. The creature crouched, readying itself to pounce.

Chapter 34 – The Formulae

Otto's heart beat in his ears and though he wanted to scream, his mouth was so dry no words could escape.

"Easy now," whispered Jethro. "No sudden moves."

But Delderfield clutched hold of the parrot and away he ran, back the way they'd come. His footsteps thundered down the tunnel.

The lion roared, even louder this time. Otto's stomach lurched. Florence's whole body visibly shook.

Otto felt himself being scooped up off his feet and before he could focus his thoughts, Jethro was sprinting with him back down the tunnel. Florence chased after them.

The lion pounced, landing just millimetres from Florence's heel. No matter how fast they ran, the lion was just a whisper behind, its well-oiled cogs spinning with each new leap.

Jethro burst out of the tunnel and back into the stone chamber, with Florence close behind. The door to the tunnel slammed shut behind them into the face of the leaping lion, mid roar.

"Welcome back, Jethro," said Emoria. "It's so very useful having a zoo, don't you think? Now Delderfield, give me that."

Delderfield huddled on the floor by the crocodile's tank, cradling the squawking parrot. The crocodile slapped the water with its tail, splashing a spray of water down onto Delderfield's head.

"There's work to be done and your patient is waiting," lectured Emoria.

The octopus loomed up above her. Delderfield let out a moan and sank his head into his hands.

Jethro lowered Otto to the floor.

"You too." Emoria beckoned Otto to where she stood. "It's a very delicate operation. I'm sure you and your uncle know what's at stake. As you can see, there is no way out of here, not for you. And when you are finished, Delderfield, you can begin enhancing the rest of my zoo."

"But..."

Otto thought of the heart that beat inside the monkey, and the parrots too. It was more than a heart, so much more. His mother's invention had created a spark of life in her mechanical creatures; they were no longer machines, they felt and thought for themselves. There were other kinds of creatures too: the octopus and the lion. They were dangerous as machines, but the possibility of them gaining the ability to make decisions, and to plan, was terrifying.

"No buts, Delderfield. My friend here is just the first. You didn't stop with one parrot, did you?"

"No, but... There's not enough, not enough to..."

"Then you shall make some more, as much as it takes to bring all my creatures to life, every single one of them." Emoria pulled Otto close and put her arm around his shoulder. She smelt of engine oil, the kind his uncle used to lubricate his creatures' joints.

Emoria took a musket out of the holster strapped around her hips. She raised it towards Otto. "Throw down your cutlass, Jethro, and your musket, then kick them over to me. Delderfield, you will do as I ask or you can say goodbye to your nephew," snapped Emoria.

"You don't understand," cried Delderfield, scrabbling to his feet. "I couldn't, even if I wanted to."

"Don't be difficult." Emoria pushed the muzzle of the musket against Otto's cheek. "It's a simple choice."

"Please!" pleaded Delderfield.

Jethro flashed him a look.

Otto shook so much he couldn't stop his teeth from chattering. "I don't have the formulae, only Natisha had that."

"Then find it. Now!" bellowed Emoria.

The musket dug into Otto's skin and he closed his eyes tight.

"But I never had it... Never seen it... Please..." babbled Delderfield.

Emoria stamped her foot. The parrot clasped under Delderfield's arm squawked. The octopus slung out a tentacle.

Otto's mind jolted back to the steam galleon and Jethro's cabin; to the drawer in his desk full of cogs and springs. He remembered the leather notebook full of numbers and symbols he couldn't understand. The formulae book lay rocking in the hull of the steam galleon moored upon the shore. Otto said nothing but his eyes met Jethro's and Jethro shook his head just a fraction as he flicked his hair out of his eyes and threw the musket to the ground. He chucked his cutlass too and kicked them both towards Emoria.

"I want those other parrots and that wretched monkey too," yelled Emoria. "You can transplant their hearts into more worthy creatures."

"No!" cried Otto.

Five mechanical parrots stayed hidden and only the monkey knew where, but of course it wasn't going to tell anybody.

Chapter 35 – Sabotage

Otto stood beside his uncle in front of four workbenches which had been pushed together to form one large operating table. Delderfield's hands shook as he laid out a tray of instruments: a spanner, a socket set, a pair of long slender forceps and a pair of tongs. By Otto's side sat the black metal box. Inside, oblivious of its final resting place, shivered the purple blog, his mother's invention.

"We shouldn't be doing this," muttered Delderfield.

"Well it wasn't my idea," hissed Otto.

"Do get a move on, Delderfield," called Emoria. She sat on an upturned wooden crate, her legs crossed at the ankle. Behind her, the parrot cage housed one crippled parrot and two new residents, Jethro and Florence.

Florence sat hunched over her notebook, a piece of charcoal in hand. Busily she sketched the octopus that lay silent and motionless upon the operating table. Its eyes stared up at the stone ceiling; its tentacles laid out long and straight. Florence smudged the charcoal to contour the creature's vast head. She drew big dots for the bolts that were soon to be removed.

"It looks like a harmless pile of junk now," said Jethro, watching over Florence's shoulder.

"We should have got hold of its key," said Florence.

But the key hung around Emoria's neck, so big and heavy it must have weighed her down. She drummed the metal with her fingers. "Not long now my darling," she said, her words unheard by the slumbering octopus that had taken several hours to wind down as Jethro had paced the parrot cage.

"You can't hurry such delicate work," grumbled Delderfield. Sweat gathered above his eyebrows. When at last he grasped the spanner, the fingers holding it trembled so much he had to hold his wrist steady with his other hand.

"You should have told me about my mother," said Otto, keeping his voice so low it was almost a whisper. "You should have told me about my father. You had no right to take me like that, that's kidnapping. You lied to me."

"I was trying to protect you." Delderfield placed the spanner around the first bolt at the base of the octopus's head.

"From what, my own father? My rightful place as a pirate?"

Delderfield turned the spanner and the rusted bolt began to shift. "You were so small, a pirate ship is no place for a child... Not without your mother."

Otto's anger bubbled and his voice grew louder. "But you never asked Jethro what he wanted."

Delderfield's hand slipped and the spanner jumped off the bolt.

"Stop chatting you two," called Emoria. "I'm watching you, so no silly mistakes."

Delderfield tried again. This time he unscrewed the bolt and removed it and started to unscrew the next.

"I was wrong, I can see that now."

Otto's uncle passed him the bolt and two more after that. Carefully, he began to remove the first metal plate that formed the base of the octopus's head.

"Me and Jethro argued when he became a pirate. I had no idea my sister had followed him to sea and when I did it was too late. I was angry... Angry of what my best friend had become... What might become of my sister."

Otto took the second metal plate and placed it beside the first. Inside the octopus's head lay a mass of wires and springs, far more complex than Otto had imagined. Somehow, all that worked to articulate the octopus's tentacles and help it hear every sound. That's when Otto had an idea.

He edged nearer to his uncle as he took hold of the third metal plate. Looking inside, Otto marvelled at the intricate system of pulleys and gears which took up much of the lower space inside the octopus's head and body. Only the upper recesses seemed empty enough to accommodate the beating purple blob. What if something went wrong?

Otto's uncle worked carefully, his long slender fingers removing each bolt and metal plate in turn with precision. He took care not to disturb the clockwork mechanism deep within the octopus's body cavity. Otto realised how terribly delicate it all looked inside its rusted exterior.

"Emoria is watching everything we do," Otto whispered. "We have no choice but to transplant the beating heart inside, but..."

His uncles fingers stopped working. "Go on."

Otto had realised something else too. No matter how angry he was with his uncle, their only hope was to work together. "You could damage something really important inside," whispered Otto so quietly he wondered if his uncle had even heard him.

Delderfield continued working but seconds later he whispered back. "You mean sabotage? It could work, but Emoria would be sure to find out... She'd kill us."

"We have to do something," hissed Otto. He wanted to kick his uncle under the table to make him see sense but Otto knew Emoria was watching every move they made. He could feel her gaze on his back, could hear her goggles whirring. "You can't let her turn this beast into a monster... A thinking monster."

Delderfield grabbed the forceps and reached deep inside of the body of the octopus. "You might be right," he breathed.

"Then it's agreed," whispered Otto.

"But I fear you may have forgotten something."

Otto looked around. Emoria sat twisting the large metal key in her hands. Behind her, Jethro stood watching through the bars and Florence sat drawing. Jethro caught Otto's gaze and gestured to the top of the parrot cage where the monkey sat.

"Keep your eyes on the operation," called Emoria. "You need to learn how this is done."

Otto turned back to the operating table. He was sure Emoria hadn't seen what he had. He took two more bolts from his uncle and leaned in closer to whisper under his breath. "The monkey has already thought of that."

"Ahh," muttered Delderfield. "I need the wire cutters over there but if I reach to get them Emoria is sure to see."

"I'll create a diversion," whispered Otto.

"I think Jethro has taught you well, or maybe it was your friend, Florence."

"I have pirate blood," smiled Otto.

"Hey, Emoria!" hollered Jethro. "We're parched over here, how about something to drink?"

Otto turned to look and in that second Jethro winked.

"Maybe you've forgotten we humans need to eat and drink." Jethro kicked the cage and rattled the bars.

Emoria spun round. "Silence, or I'll have your brain replaced with cogs!"

Before Delderfield had a chance to react, Otto reached over and grabbed the wire cutters. He secreted them up his sleeve. Delderfield kept working, his nimble fingers removing the last metal panel. Somehow with all the clockwork exposed, the octopus suddenly looked very vulnerable.

"Do hurry up Delderfield," called Emoria. "Your friends are getting restless. Dawdling won't put off the inevitable, so you may as well get on with it."

The monkey crept down the front of the cage. The parrot didn't make a sound.

"If you're so impatient, Emoria," called Delderfield, "Maybe you should do this yourself."

Otto slipped the wire cutters to his uncle.

Emoria laughed. "Oh no, Delderfield, that's why I have you."

Soundlessly the monkey broke into the lock with a piece of wire. Jethro and Florence watched him do it but of course they didn't say a word. Emoria's goggles were firmly fixed on Delderfield.

Delderfield reached the wire cutters deep inside the octopus. Otto saw his uncle's leg tremble, so too his hand. A drip of sweat landed on the bristles of his moustache. Somewhere inside, the wire cutters hit metal and the sound echoed in the hollow cavity.

Otto's heart missed a beat.

Emoria sprang up so quickly she knocked over the wooden crate she'd been sitting on. She lunged towards Delderfield and grabbed

141

him on the shoulder. The wire cutters slipped from his hand and clattered deep inside the octopus.

"You deceitful pile of human waste!" screeched Emoria. "Get off of him, what are you trying to do?" Emoria pulled Delderfield away from the operating table just as the parrot cage clicked open and Jethro stepped free.

A terrific squawking rang out. Five mechanical parrots swept across the chamber above Emoria's head. Otto saw a flash of the metal key hanging around Emoria's neck and he reached out to grab it.

"No you don't!" screamed Emoria. She pushed Otto so hard he crumpled up against the operating table and slid to the floor.

Emoria scrambled up onto the table and straddled the octopus. She slid the key into the side of the octopus's head and furiously began to wind.

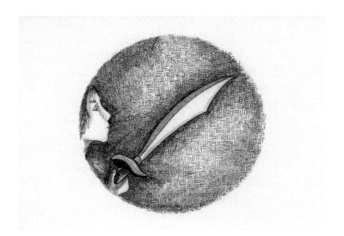

Chapter 36 – A Memory Reborn

As Emoria wound the key, the octopus's tentacles began to twitch. Otto rubbed his head and staggered away from the operating table. Delderfield stood in a daze, his head in his hands, his shoulders shaking. Otto realised his uncle was sobbing, his chest heaving with each breath.

"You'll be sorry you tried to trick me," snarled Emoria.

Florence stuffed her notebook back inside her dress and hurried after Jethro, the broken parrot wedged under her arm. Parrots swept around the chamber, squawking in unison. Repeatedly they swooped at Emoria. They pecked her hair and clipped her body with their wings but she wouldn't stop winding until the octopus stretched out a tentacle and flicked it high in the air, scattering the parrots to each far corner of the chamber.

Otto staggered towards Jethro and Florence. The monkey jumped up onto Otto's shoulder and wrapped its tail tightly around his neck. Florence gently took Delderfield's hand and pulled him along. The four of them sprinted towards the doorway.

As the parrots re-grouped, Emoria clambered down to the floor. "You're not going anywhere!" she bellowed, stamping her foot.

Behind her, the parrots flew at the octopus like an orchestrated squadron. Jethro marched out through the doorway and past the crocodile tank. Florence pounded on the control panel on the wall, just as Emoria had done and the metal elevator doors pinged open. Otto's heart lifted. Maybe they really could just walk out. Delderfield was sullen and silent and Otto guessed there was nothing left to say.

Behind them Otto heard Emoria scream and curse. Having switched their attention to Emoria, the parrots' squawks were deafening. The octopus dragged itself forwards.

"In you go," said Jethro, pushing Delderfield into the elevator before him. Florence slipped in beside him and Otto jumped in after them. Jethro had just put one foot inside when he was whisked out of the elevator and winched high into the air.

Delderfield wailed.

"Put him down!" yelled Florence.

In horror, Otto saw his father dangling above them, a tentacle wrapped tightly around his left ankle. A cold sweat ran down Otto's neck. Florence slammed the button on the wall but as the metal doors began to close, a tentacle whipped between them. It was followed by a second. With a terrible wrenching of metal, the octopus clawed the doors open.

Otto's heart pounded so fast he fought to breath. Outside the elevator, Jethro thrashed around, suspended upside down in the air with his arms flailing around him. His cutlass slipped out of his boot and clattered to the floor below. His mane of black curls swayed like a rope.

"I told you there was no escape!" roared a jubilant Emoria. She dodged the dive bombing parrots. Weaving in and out she ran towards where the octopus dangled Jethro like a small toy.

Otto's head began to spin. He could hear what sounded like the crashing of the ocean in his ears. His vision blurred. Jethro's wails turned into the laughter of his mother, then to her screams and for a second it was no longer Jethro suspended in the air but his mother. She was screaming his name. The floor beneath Otto swayed like a ship on the crest of a wave. He stumbled and sank to his knees. This couldn't be happening, not again, not Jethro.

Emoria howled with laughter, drowning out the cries of Jethro who wriggled and writhed in the air.

Florence crawled out of the elevator and grabbed the cutlass from the floor. Repeatedly, she slashed at the octopus. "Let him go! Let him down!" The more she danced around the more Emoria roared with laughter.

Otto opened his mouth to cry out but in that second the octopus uncurled its tentacle, releasing its hold on Jethro's ankle.

Otto's screams were silent as Jethro fell, fruitlessly waving his arms in the air until he crashed to the floor with a sickening thud.

Chapter 37 - The Seed of an Idea

Jethro lay on the floor, his left leg twisted beneath him. The parrots circled above him, squawking loudly.

Emoria stood with her hands on her hips. "Whoops!"

"Look what you've done," uttered Delderfield, his face ashen, his hands trembling.

Otto scrambled over to where his father lay and threw his arms around him.

"So very touching, don't you think, Delderfield? Your sister's child, so attached to a notorious steam pirate. Just what you've been trying to prevent all these years."

"You could have killed him," exclaimed Florence, joining Otto, down on her knees.

"Just like..." stammered Delderfield.

Emoria pulled Delderfield up by the arm. "Back to work."

"You can't just leave him here," cried Otto.

Jethro winced.

"His leg's broken," shouted Florence.

"I warned you," snapped Emoria. "Now back to the operating table."

Emoria tried to drag Delderfield along but he dug in his heels.

"No!"

"You will do as I say or I'll..."

"Or you'll what?" said Delderfield. He tugged his arm away and stooped down to Jethro's side. "You'll have your monster kill us all?"

Emoria's goggles zoomed out. The octopus reached a tentacle out towards where Delderfield stood but Emoria grabbed hold of it and flung it away.

"I don't need to. I only need to kill the young pirate here." She raised her musket and pointed it to where Otto sat hugging his father. "Or this little monkey."

Otto's heart missed a beat. He swung round to see the octopus towering above them, the monkey dangling from one of its tentacles. The monkey's porcelain teeth chattered.

"No!" cried Otto.

"Well Delderfield, are you ready?"

Otto's eyes pleaded with his uncle. Delderfield's moustache twitched. Jethro opened his mouth to speak.

"Silence Jethro. I wasn't asking you," cut in Emoria.

Delderfield lowered himself to the floor and there he sat with his arms folded. "I won't help you, not anymore."

The monkey screeched.

"But uncle..." Otto pointed up at the monkey that twisted helplessly in the octopus's grip.

Delderfield shook his head.

Jethro squeezed Otto's hand.

"I'll do it," said Otto.

His uncle looked up.

"You can't..." began Florence.

"Let the monkey down and I'll transplant the heart into the octopus. I can do it, I know I can," pleaded Otto.

Delderfield stared open mouthed at Otto. "How can you do such a thing... After what... What it's done... What it did to your...?"

Otto couldn't bear to think of his mother again or picture the scene. He had a plan, a seed of an idea which began to sprout and grow. He winked up at the monkey. Only the monkey had an inkling of what Otto was thinking but it wouldn't have told anyone, even if it could.

Emoria's goggles whirred and zoomed out to focus on Otto's face. She grabbed hold of one of the octopus's tentacles and shook it. "Drop it," she shouted.

Delderfield shuffled over to where Otto now stood. "What are you doing? This is madness," he hissed.

But Otto knew exactly what he was doing and the way he saw it, it was their only hope. The octopus released the monkey and Otto waited with open arms to catch it.

"Delderfield, prepare the operating table."

Otto's uncle shook his head. "I'll have nothing to do with it."

"I don't need his help," piped up Otto, hugging the monkey. "The monkey will be my assistant."

Jethro flashed Otto a look but Otto turned away.

It was getting late when finally the octopus once more lay lifelessly stretched out on the operating table. Delderfield had joined Jethro and Florence back in the cage with the broken parrot. The other five parrots roosted out of Emoria's reach and she was far too busy getting the octopus ready to care. Otto was reassured by their presence. He was sure they had sensed the urgency of his furtive whispers to the monkey.

Delderfield had insisted on straightening Jethro's broken leg, strapping it to a metal rod in an attempt to keep it straight. Otto had wanted to talk to his father to try to explain but Emoria strictly kept them apart.

"You've chosen your path Otto, seen more sense than those three put together. It seems you are now my new assistant. But don't even think about tricking me again or I'll throw your friends to the lion, along with that mischievous monkey of yours."

Otto had kept the monkey close and had whispered his plan slowly and repeatedly until he was sure the monkey understood. Even so the wait had made Otto nervous. So nervous that a swarm of butterflies danced in his stomach and his heartbeat drummed in his ears every time he looked at the octopus. Motionless, the monster lay before him, its inner workings exposed. Otto kept glancing at the creature's glazed eyes that stared blankly up at the stone ceiling, checking they didn't flicker with life. In front of him sat the purple blob that his mother had invented, beating with life beside a pair of forceps all lined up ready for the transplant.

Otto daren't swallow, his mouth was so dry. He could feel his uncle's resentment in every glance he shot him. Otto grasped the forceps in his shaking hand and clenched the purple mass tightly between the two metal scoops. He could see the disappointment in Florence's face. Otto lifted the forceps and carefully guided them deep inside the body cavity of the octopus. Only Jethro smiled weakly, so clearly in pain.

Emoria was ecstatic. She clapped her hands loudly as Otto began to attach the purple mass to wires deep inside the slumbering octopus.

"Oh my darling, it won't be long," she cried.

Otto's hand trembled. What if he'd made a terrible mistake?

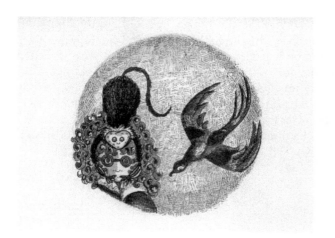

Chapter 38 – The Octopus Awakes

The operation was complete. Deep inside the octopus beat a purple heart, sending a spark of life down all its connected wires. They buzzed as the life force raced through every part of the creature's metal body. Otto's heart beat faster. Fear fizzed through his veins. He looked at the monkey and nodded.

Otto turned to face Emoria. "It's done," he said, trying to keep his voice from betraying him. "Give me the key and I'll wind up the octopus." He reached out his hand. What if Emoria refused? He held his arm rigid to stop it trembling and with as much confidence as he could muster he waited. "This is a delicate moment," he lied. "I need to be sure I've connected it correctly."

If Emoria wavered, it was only for a second. Her eyes blazed with excitement. Any minute now her beloved octopus would awake with a beating heart and with it, free will and a mind of its own. Otto knew free will could be a dangerous thing. He was relying upon it.

Emoria thrust the key into Otto's outstretched hand. The monkey waited. Otto crawled up onto the operating table and quickly inserted the key before Emoria could change her mind. His fingers felt weak. Behind him his uncle wailed.

"Stop!" shouted Florence, rattling the bars of the cage. "Don't do it."

But Otto carried on winding. With each rotation of the key the octopus twitched. Its eyes snapped open and its tentacles shifted. The life force surged through the octopus with such power that the mechanical beast jolted up off the bench, knocking Otto over.

In that second the monkey screeched and launched itself at Emoria, who clearly wasn't expecting it as she let out a terrific scream. The monkey landed on her head, amongst her red curls and clasped its hands around her neck. It giggled loudly and appeared to plant a kiss on Emoria's cheek. The octopus swung its tentacles across the floor of the chamber. On cue the parrots flew down from their perch and Otto held his breath. The monkey went to kiss her again only this time it bit down hard on Emoria's ear.

"Arghhhhh!" shrieked Emoria. She grabbed the monkey by the leg and flung it over her head, sending it sailing through the air. It landed with a thud on the floor and lay there, sprawled in a heap, arms splayed around it. It was silent and still.

Although Otto had been expecting it, he couldn't help but cry out.

Emoria was so enraged, she raised her foot above the helpless monkey as if to stamp on it tiny chest and in so doing she sealed her fate.

"Do something!" shouted Florence.

Otto's uncle hid his head in his hands and Jethro raised an eyebrow. But Otto did nothing, he had to let it play out. He prayed he wasn't wrong, with every ounce of his being.

Five parrots swooped at Emoria, so close that she almost lost her balance. She threw out her arms and with remarkable ease, she grabbed one of the parrots by its tail feathers. The injured parrot, still nestled on Delderfield's lap, let out a deafening squawk.

The octopus paused and stared; first at Emoria and then at the parrot she dangled in her hand. Then, she casually tossed it down, to join the monkey on the floor.

"Now come here my darling," called Emoria, striding across to where the octopus sat watching her. "Let's not let these creatures ruin our special moment."

The octopus narrowed its eyes. Emoria reached out her hand towards it but before her fingers could touch its cold metal, a tentacle wrapped itself like a chain tightly around her wrist.

"What...?" Emoria's eyes widened and the first sign of panic flickered within.

Otto eased past the octopus, who only had eyes for Emoria. He raced over to the cage where Jethro hauled himself up and Florence was pointing excitedly. She nudged Delderfield to look.

The octopus grabbed Emoria round first one, then both ankles, and whipped her off the floor.

"Put me down... I...," she wailed, her words sucked away by shock.

The parrots squawked. Emoria looked over to where the monkey still lay, pretending to be broken and the realisation must have hit. "It's not... They'll be fine... I wouldn't... I only meant to..."

But the octopus, who was sure to be listening, ignored her cries. It dragged Emoria kicking and screaming out of the chamber.

Jethro met Otto's gaze and burst out laughing. "You planned this, didn't you? You sly pirate!"

Otto sank down beside his father and smiled through the bars. "Well, she did want the octopus to think for itself. It looks like it's done just that."

As the octopus dragged Emoria away, the sound of metal upon stone reverberated throughout the chamber.

"I wonder what it will do?" marvelled Delderfield, colour once more blushed across his cheeks. Even his moustache had spring in it again.

The monkey scrambled up off the floor and took a bow. Beside it, the parrot flapped its wings in triumph.

Otto stood on the beach looking out to sea. Jethro, his leg securely strapped, stood supported by Delderfield and Florence. The broken parrot lay tucked inside an improvised bag slung over Florence's shoulder. Out in the bay the octopus lowered Emoria beneath the cresting waves. Five mechanical parrots circled above Otto's head, keeping at bay an army of watching crabs.

"Not quite the love she was expecting," said Delderfield. "It's a shame the octopus holds the last of my sister's invention."

"You could make some more," said Otto.

"Believe me Otto, over the years I have tried to recreate it in vain," said his uncle. "Without her formulae it just can't be done."

"I know where it is," said Otto. He watched the octopus bobbing up and down in the waves. "My mother's formulae book is in the steam galleon, it's been there all along."

The monkey, who sat on Otto's shoulder, clapped excitedly.

"What about Emoria?" said Florence.

The octopus had disappeared beneath the surface of the sea taking Emoria with it. Fathoms beneath the Pantatlantic ocean lay a rust encrusted parrot on the ocean bed. The mechanical parrot hadn't stirred since that fateful day on the steam galleon. Emoria Cogwright dropped through the water, her red curls splayed out like a mermaid, her eyes wide open. She could no longer see the shoal of fish that swam around her. But if the parrot saw her, it would never tell.

Chapter 39 – Otto's Farewell

Florence sat in the orangery with her notebook open on her lap. Deftly she swept green paint across the page forming leaves to join the parrots already painted in the branches of a tree. Beside her, silver fish swam between paddling flamingos in a babbling stream. A flurry of clouds floated out of the cloud machine. Above her six mechanical parrots squawked their approval.

"Are you really going to paint that on the wall of my uncle's factory?" asked Otto. He stood watching his friend. All Otto cared about sat packed into a small knapsack beside his feet. The monkey squatted on top, a spotted handkerchief knotted around its neck.

"Sure, it'll look great. I might even paint the sea too."

"You ready?" called Jethro. The steam pirate leaned onto a wooden crutch under his arm, though his leg had all but healed already. "Wish we could see it finished, Florence, but I've been on land long enough and the sea beckons. We could always do with another crew member if you change your mind."

"Leave my new job?" said Florence. "No way. Anyway, I'm not sure I'm cut out to be a pirate, not like Otto."

Jethro hugged his son. Around Otto's neck hung his mother's pendant and he rubbed it between his fingers. Being on the steam galleon had brought back so many memories of her; snatches of her smile and her laughter too. The sea was where he belonged, he knew that now.

"Just keep out of trouble," called Delderfield.

Otto's uncle stood in the doorway, a mechanical pelican tucked under his arm that wriggled with impatience. "I may have persuaded the Brigade to let you sail but it's on the condition you never sail into Brummington again, Jethro."

"I'll miss you," said Otto. "Both of you."

Jethro winked at Florence. "Since when have I ever obeyed the rules," he laughed. "We'll be back, just you wait and see."

"I'll take care of your room for you," said Florence, daubing yellow spots for lemons between the leaves. "It'll take a bit of getting used to sleeping in a bed again."

"Well I can't have my new factory supervisor squatting in a derelict building," said Delderfield. "With this position comes respectability and with that, certain standards to uphold. And anyway, now I am your official guardian, and this is your home."

Florence held out the finished painting. "What do you think?"

"Perfect," said Delderfield.

The monkey clapped.

Otto would miss Florence terribly. For the last few weeks they had helped his uncle build a new mechanical workforce to run his factory. There were orangutans to operate the weaving looms, mice to collect the dropped threads from the floor and a rather spectacular octopus to thread the looms. The octopus had been Florence's idea. At first, Delderfield argued against it but even he had to admit that eight tentacles were very useful indeed and anyway this octopus was small, purple and meticulously careful. Otto wondered whatever happened to Emoria's octopus. He liked to imagine it was looking after the rest of the mechanical zoo on Gostopolus Island, though he had no intention of finding out.

"The very first fully mechanized factory," chuckled Jethro. "Natisha would have been proud. Quite the talk of the town. Carry on like this and we won't recognise the place next time we steam into port."

Florence shut her notebook, tucked it back inside her dress and jumped up. "I'm coming to wave you off," she cried.

Delderfield put down the struggling pelican, reached up into a palm tree and scooped down one of the parrots. He held it out to Otto. "A pirate needs a parrot," he said. The parrot flew up onto Otto's shoulder and there it perched, squawking in agreement.

"And a pirate needs a friend too," said Jethro, taking Delderfield's hand firmly. Otto's uncle smiled but he couldn't hide the tears which made his eyes glisten.

Down at the harbour a crowd had gathered. Otto stood aboard the steam galleon with Jethro. A brilliant blue sky made the water in the harbour sparkle. Florence balanced on the sea wall, joined by Ginger, Spud and Blinker. Ginger waved furiously. Spud and Blinker whistled.

"Don't forget us!" called Ginger, as the steam galleon left its mooring. Ginger's hair was a blaze of auburn in the sun.

The parrot sat on Jethro's shoulder and the monkey settled down in the crow's nest. A lump stuck in Otto's throat. How could he ever forget them? Without them, he wouldn't be sailing away with his father, happier than he had ever been. Otto watched Brummington slip away into the distance, and his new life as a pirate began.

The End

Other books for young people available from Stairwell Books

Ivy Elf's Magical Mission	Elisabeth Kelly
The Pirate Queen	Charlie Hill
Harriet the Elephotamus	Fiona Kirkman
A Business of Ferrets	Alwyn Bathan
Shadow Cat Summer	Rebecca Smith
Very Bad Gnus	Suzanne Sheran
The Water Bailiff's Daughter	Yvonne Hendrie
Season of the Mammoth	Antony Wootten
The Grubby Feather Gang	Antony Wootten
Mouse Pirate	Dawn Treacher
Rosie and John's Magical Adventure	The Children of Ryedale District Primary Schools

For further information please contact rose@stairwellbooks.com

www.stairwellbooks.co.uk
@stairwellbooks